Andrew Cotto

Black Irish Blues

Black Rose Writing | Texas

ISBN: 978-1-68433-615-9
PUBLISHED BY BLACK ROSE WRITING
www.blackrosewriting.com

Printed in the United States of America
Suggested Retail Price (SRP) $16.95

Black Irish Blues is printed in Georgia

*As a planet-friendly publisher, Black Rose Writing does its best to eliminate
unnecessary waste to reduce paper usage and energy costs, while never compromising
the reading experience. As a result, the final word count vs. page count may not meet
common expectations.

This book is very much informed by the town of Glen Rock, NJ; and I'd like to dedicate it to the townspeople I know and especially to the families Mangini, Ferrari, and O'Shea.

Acknowledgments

I'd like to thank my family, friends and supporters of my writing over the years. Drumming up interest in a book is harder than writing them, so I am deeply appreciative of your continued presence in my writing life.

I'm also appreciative of Black Rose Writing for making something real out of what otherwise only exists within my imagination (and my hard drive). Finally, thanks to Virginia Valenzuela for the thorough editing and counsel.

Black Irish Blues

Prologue

The trouble with Dinny Tuite began with the two-martini rule. It was an axiom of sorts about drinking and limits, shared often by my mother, that I thought to share with Dinny Tuite who was sitting on two martinis, thinking about a third. He'd come into my barroom on an autumn afternoon. The plantation shades were slanted over the wide windows that faced the west, and the fuzzy sunshine slatted the planks to fill the dark room with diffuse light.

Dinny ordered a straight-up, bone-dry, Stoli martini, no olives. He had a way of speaking I couldn't make: slick but mannered, unusual, like his name. He kept his money on the bar in a chrome clip and wore a sharp suit, tailored to his lithe frame; he was young, about my age, late 20s but all grown up, troubled-actor handsome, a dimple in his chin and an active Adam's apple; a head of flowing black hair and green eyes. They called his type black Irish, back when I was a kid, back when there were a lot more Irish descendants in this town; and though I hadn't been around in a dozen years or so, I knew he wasn't from around here at all, not from the 1st generation Irish or Italians who raised their kids in the trappings of 1970s, lower-middle class suburbia: Catholic schools and Police Athletic Leagues and CYO, and two weeks every summer at the Jersey shore or someplace upstate. At least for some.

It wasn't like that for me and mine at all. Our family was a disaster. I was the youngest son of no-good Timothy Stiles and his tragic Italian wife, refugees, both, from the Bronx and victims of a cursed ancestry. They had three boys, two dead now, with the last - me - responsible in some way for the respective deaths of both brothers. And I'd run away from this town at the age of 15 because of the first and good brother dying, and I was back and free all these years later because of the very recent death of the other one, which didn't bother me at all.

I'd spent the years away rambling around America, hopping trains and hitching rides, cooking or tending bar or building houses, never in one place for too long, except the years just spent in Brooklyn, close enough to home in northern Jersey, but not too close, until it was safe to move back into the abandoned house I'd grown up in and buy my hometown's only Inn to refurbish and redeem and make my own, and hopefully end my family's curse.

I bought the place in the spring and shut it down as the heat arrived, spending the summer sweating through my clothes in the undertaking of a massive gutting and rehab that turned a forever dingy watering hole with crap food and the ancient stench of broken drunks - including my own father - into a respectable establishment with plenty of light, a welcoming atmosphere, and damn good things to eat. We'd reopened a few weeks after Labor Day, and I'd dedicated most of my time to operations and the kitchen; I left the bar to the old-schooler who'd worked there since nearly before I was born 28 years earlier.

Richie the bartender, after his first summer off since quitting high school at age 16, had enjoyed his long days reading Raymond Chandler novels and lounging around his cottage by Greenwood Lake, just across the border into New York State. He talked about not coming back to work at all, after feeling his body recover from 40 years standing behind a bar, first in his native Bronx and then here. Richie agreed to stay on for shortened hours, a no-smoking rule anywhere within the premises, two nights a week off, and whatever he wanted from my new menu (whether he was working or not).

The afternoon that I met Dinny Tuite, Richie was on the schedule to tend, and he sat at the end of the bar in the natural light immersed in savory aroma and mopping up the sauce of the chicken dish he'd ordered for the second evening in a row: brined thighs, broiled then covered in a sauce bright with lemon, olive oil, garlic, and oregano. Richie was the only one in the joint, besides me and Dinny Tuite, who was sitting on two martinis, thinking about a third.

"You know what my mother used to say about martinis?" I asked him.

He set his green eyes on me, and they pulsed for a beat before he decided to engage the tall stranger behind the bar in a white t-shirt with lank, brown hair pulled into a tight pony tail, and a large German knife paused from dicing fruit.

We locked eyes until a small smile creased his face and he spoke in a bemused tone.

"No, no. Tell me. Wha'd your mother used say about martinis?"

I put the knife down, wiped my hands and leaned into the bar, toward the man who needed to know the two Martini rule.

"They're like boobs," I said. "One's not enough, but three are too many."

His face went to work registering the comment, squints and smirks and tilts to both sides as he tried to figure if he'd been insulted or enlightened. It was like waiting for a slot machine to reveal its outcome, and I could tell this guy had a lot of potential outcomes, coiled and complex beneath the preternatural ease. He sniffed and straightened on his stool, and I sensed an insult forming, possibly one that involved my mother. And that would be bad.

Richie cleared his throat and made some music with his silverware and plate. Dinny Tuite looked down at him and nodded before setting his eyes back on me just as I spun the big knife handle three times around my palm and buried the blade into a wooden cutting board. The 5:45 commuter train rolled into the station with a loud blast of its horn.

"Know how to use a knife?" he asked once the silence returned.

"I do."

"Cut some people?"

"I have."

He nodded and breathed through his nose, looked down at Richie and then back at me.

"And where are you from?" I asked.

"South Philly," he answered.

I removed the blade from the cutting board, checked for damage to the tip. Dinny Tuite cleared his throat.

"You're the guy they've been talking about," he said. "The runaway, who came back and fixed this place up."

"I am."

"Did a nice job."

"Thanks."

"Why?"

"Why what?"

"Why would you want to come back here?" he asked. "This town sucks."

"You don't say?"

He polished off his drink and put the glass in front of me. I put it to the side.

Dinny Tuite sucked his teeth and stood to leave. "Your mother, with her rule about martinis, she's dead. Right?"

"Yeah," I said, feeling the sear of clever cruelty and the ache of sorrow.

"Thought so," he said.

Dinny Tuite pulled a Marlboro Light from the inside of his suit jacket, banged the filter thrice on the bar then tucked it between two long fingers. I waited for a match to appear before having to inform him that smoking was no longer allowed anywhere on the premises, though I gathered he knew that already by the way he checked with Richie before eyeballing me until his face softened and the intensity in his eyes receded. He slipped the smoke behind his ear, pulled a crisp $20 from his clip and dropped it down on a $12 tab.

"Sorry about your mother," he said. "Straight up."

I watched him glide out the door.

Richie took his plate to the kitchen and came behind the bar, tying his signature red apron over the rounded midriff of his white dress shirt over black slacks, the downy white hair still left on his head slicked back above his ears.

"And what's his story?" I asked.

"Good question," Richie said with a huff, the hardscrabble of the Bronx still present in his throat. "Name's Dinny Tuite. Married to one of the Donaghy girls."

I remembered the Donaghy girls: four blondes, each two years apart, with smiling eyes and easy laughs; the kind of girls that owned every room they were in; the kind of girls made for cheerleader outfits and wedding dresses, stars of high school yearbooks. The kind of girls that made all kinds of boys do stupid, stupid shit.

"Which one he marry?" I asked.

"The one with shit taste in men," Richie said.

"He come in a lot?"

"On occasion. Always about this time. Catches a decent buzz and splits before the regulars show."

"He trouble?"

"Not really. It's just that he don't, you know, fit in. That's all."

"Black Irish," I said. "Don't see them very much anymore."

"More black than Irish," Richie said with another huff.

"What's that mean?"

"You'll see," he said and started racking glasses.

I looked at the spot where Dinny Tuite had sat and tried to make sense of what Richie just said. All I knew was that I didn't like it, not the casual racism nor the caustic implication, but Richie was right about one thing: I'd be finding out about Dinny Tuite, though I'd never see him in my bar again.

Chapter 1

I'd only been home for a few days when a visitor from the local police department found me on the roof. The house had been in neglect for years, the years since my father ran off and my good brother died, followed by my escape into America and my awful brother going to jail. My mother had been alone all that time, the last few months dying in the house she could never make a home, despite her good will and intentions. I'd come back from my travels when she told me she was sick, but there was nothing I could do but sit with her and offer comfort. When she died, I buried her alone, but I couldn't stay in the house yet, not with so many memories and ghosts, so I boarded up the house and went to find a home in the mysteries of Brooklyn - the place where my family's history in America began.

After more than a year in Brooklyn and a week as an amateur and somehow successful detective, I realized the Borough of Kings would never be my home. A fortuitous real estate deal on the dawn of Brooklyn's gentrification filled my pockets, and a dangerous (and bloody) gamble got my baleful brother back in jail, for what was to be many, many years, so I finally felt comfortable returning to the now abandoned house where I'd grown up. I had kept the grounds in decent shape while caring for my mother and on occasional visits out from the city, but the interior and exterior needed care, particularly a leak in the roof that emptied into the front vestibule.

Second to last house on a dead-end, it was a two-story A-frame, brick around the base and aluminum siding up top. Non-distinct in a very suburban manner, built not to impress but to draw at a reasonable price, middle-class white folks from the city in the '70s. Driveway down one side, patch of grass out front and a big lot in back that ran towards the dirt road and gully behind, with fields and hills and a cookie factory beyond that billowed sugary smoke into the open sky. From the roof, over the oaks that lined the streets, you could see the Manhattan skyline in the distance and the immediate ramparts that fortressed the small neighborhood of similar houses: the dirt road behind, the electrical plant to the side, and the train tracks that sequestered the neighborhood's far side and gave it its ignominious name: the other side of the tracks.

I grew up with that stigma, along with a crew of derelicts and misfits and rebels - sons of mostly dead-beat dads and desperate moms - who spanned a generation of 1970s suburban anti-pastoral. None of us gave a shit about the neighborhood's bad name; in fact, it was a badge of honor for most. Better than being some mama's boy or a rich kid from the other side of town, though, I imagine, those loved and cared for found themselves far more secure in adulthood than those of us who walked through childhood and into adolescence with a chip on our shoulder and a steady sense of being less.

As I sat on my roof, taking a break from patching the leak, I wondered about my childhood pack. My mother, through her frequent letters, had occasionally offered updates: So and so went to jail; this one joined the army; that one threw himself off the George Washington Bridge. It was rarely good news. I didn't really care about any of them too much, except Mike McBride. We were the same age, born a couple days apart, and of the same ilk, just preternaturally in sync with each other; and - despite the acrimony between our respective families (his being of the more upstanding variety) - hardly a day went by my entire childhood and adolescence that we weren't together. We even lost our virginity on the same day, the summer we turned 14, as a fortuitous pool hopping excursion on the good side of town led us into the backyard of two older, bored girls in bathing suits.

I hadn't been in touch with Mike at all since I'd run away. Writing letters to friends was not normal back then, or at least not for us, and I knew his mother would hang up on me if I ever called their house, so I'd only imagine what my old friend was up to until my mother told me that he'd moved out west to join the Los Angeles Police Department. I wished she'd told me earlier; I could have found him during my travels.

None of the other neighborhood kids were around either, at least as far as I could tell, and the neighborhood had clearly upgraded, with two, shiny cars in most driveways and updated facades on the homes, well-kept lawns and very little noise. There were kids, but they played in the backyards, as opposed to up front or in the street. I was trying to put old names with rooftops when I saw the cop car enter the neighborhood through its only entrance, catty corner from my house in the far reaches. The small neighborhood had only one way in or out and three unofficial blocks: big block, middle block, little block. A car could run straight on the straight block parallel to the railroad tracks past a dozen houses, past the middle block, to where the entry street teed-out, and take a right on the little block, past Mike's house, halfway down six houses on either side, to the very bottom of the big block and my house, second from the dead-end, from where you'd go right, past the bottom end of the middle block, and swoop up to the spot where you entered. It wasn't an exact circle, more like a ladle, but that's how it functioned.

The cop car took that route just described, parallel to the tracks, banging a right on Mike's block and traveling slowly under a canopy of oak trees that had grown so much since I'd left, directly to my house where it parked in front. A young man with a crew cut and freckles stepped out of the car in a crisp navy uniform, shiny badge, and full arsenal on his belt. He held a hat ceremoniously under his left arm as he approached my front door. He blinked and breathed and rang the buzzer. I raised from the roof; sweat released in streams down my shirtless back, with my ponytail sticking to my spine. I envied the kid's crew cut.

"Help you?" I asked.

The young man looked around, startled, before finding me looming over the gutters above the front door.

"Afternoon, sir," he said in an officious tone. He looked fresh out of college, and just so fresh in general that any seriousness of his uniform and demeanor was undermined as he squinted up at me with the sun directly overhead. I assumed he was in the wrong place.

3

"Are you Mr. Caesar Stiles?"

I nodded, now curious. The sun slapped across my shoulders.

"Could I ask you to come down from the roof, sir?"

"What for?"

"I have an important matter to discuss with you, sir."

"Define important."

"I was sent directly by order of Sergeant McBride."

My heart flopped over once and my knees gave a little. I squatted down so as not to stagger off the roof. "Mike McBride?"

"Yes, sir. Sgt. Michael McBride sent me to see you. He would have come himself, but he's at a law enforcement conference in Baltimore."

"Wait a minute. Mike McBride is the sergeant of this town's police department?"

"Well, sir, he's a sergeant, not the sergeant."

"Since when?" I asked, way more interested in the presence of my friend than any serious matter at hand. "I thought he was in LA?"

"He returned from Los Angeles a year ago."

"Why?"

"I'm not aware of that, sir."

I pointed up the street. "Does he still live in the house where he grew up?"

"That, sir, I do not know. What I do know is that he asked me personally to discuss a very serious matter with you."

"And what's that?"

"It involves your brother, sir. Salvatore Stiles."

"What about him?"

I had risked my life to get my thick and vicious brother back in jail, and now I feared he'd found a way out again, which would probably mean the death of me. My mouth went hot and dry.

The young officer secured his hat under his arm and straightened his already straight posture. He looked dead into the sun and spoke with formality, as if rehearsed.

"Sir, I'm sorry to inform you that your brother, Salvatore Stiles, has died as of 4:35 pm yesterday at Northern State Prison."

I didn't believe it, though I believed it. I kind of always thought of Sallie as tough to kill, if not impossible.

"How? How'd he die?"

"Multiple stab wounds."

"Someone stabbed him?"

"Someones, sir. He was jumped by a group of men, apparently. One of them, also, was killed in the exchange."

That made sense. I couldn't imagine Sallie going down easy. He'd almost managed to kill me a few weeks before with two very large cops all over him. Not a shred of remorse pulsed through me. He brutalized my life; he ran off my father and made my mother sick with worry. I hated his guts, and I was glad he was dead. A burden felt lifted and life seemed new. That's how I thought about it at the time, but it would turn out that my malevolent brother could still cause me pain and put me in danger, even from the grave.

Chapter 2

A few days later, none other than Mike McBride himself walked into my barroom. The Inn's purchase had finally been made official, the keys provided and the town's only liquor license secured. It would be a dry town for as long as I renovated, so I vowed to get the job done fast. I'd spent the previous day clearing all the old furniture and shitty decor out the back into a dumpster in the parking lot.

The next morning was dedicated to packing up all the booze under and behind the bar, so I could give the nicked and worn bar top a proper sanding and clean mahogany stain. I was loading up the last case of booze when a familiar voice came through the back door and into the barroom.

"Whad'ya say, Caes?" It was Mike, with the breathless giggle that informed his greetings.

He had the same, round and smooth Irish face, bright blue eyes and soft sandy hair, cut even shorter for law enforcement purposes, but his upper body had ballooned through the shoulders and chest as if he'd swallowed a tire sideways and it settled below his neck. He'd always been into fitness and had started lifting weights in junior high, but I'd never imagine him this big.

"Christ all mighty," I said. "You been lifting?"

"A little bit," he said with the deprecation I was glad he still practiced.

He walked right up in his dark uniform and gave me a hug that set a ripple of pops down my spine and lifted me off the ground. I was still taller than Mike, but it didn't feel that way any longer. He put me down and took a step back to look me over in my sleeveless white t-shirt and torn blue jeans.

"You been getting your swell on a little, too, eh?"

It felt weird, staring at a face so familiar, so intimate, but having not set eyes on in a dozen some years, though it could have been yesterday. Time felt moot, and I realized how baffling it would be to be home and how ageless real friendship was. I also realized how often I'd been lonely and in need of a friend.

"So, tough guy, how ya been?" Mike asked.

"Not bad. You?"

"Can't complain. Sorry about Sallie."

"OK," I said.

"Didn't think you'd be sorry, but you might be."

"And how's that?"

"Tell you later." Mike looked around the bar. "Always hated this place. What a shit hole."

Mike had no direct relationship to the Inn, but he knew what dive bars did to certain families. He was like that.

"Yeah," I agreed.

"Gonna fix it up good?"

"Hope so."

"Good."

"Could use some muscles, Muscles."

"Sorry, Caes. No time, but I could bring some guys over. I pass a corner of Chicanos on my way to work."

"Here in town?"

"Nah," Mike laughed. "No laborers hanging around here these days. I live over in Emerest. On the way to work, I pass a corner where Chicanos wait in an empty lot each morning, looking for labor."

"Why'd you come back from LA?"

Mike smiled and then his face went flat.

"What are you doing tonight?" he asked.

I shrugged.

"Good. I'll pick you up at your house after I get off, at seven. Take you out for a welcome back dinner, a few drinks. We can catch up, and I'll tell you what you should know about your brother. Sound good?"

"Yeah," I said. "Sounds good."

Though it sounded even better than that.

Chapter 3

I'd been ambivalent about being home, but the idea of doing something as simple as going to dinner with an old friend - to catch up on lost time and do some reminiscing - had me feeling good about this move. My mother had believed our family was cursed because her mother - who had come to America from Sicily not to immigrate and make a life, but to kill a man - sent our family spinning into tragedies, which were fostered by a sense of movement and escape. Before she died, she had begged me to find a home, to make a life and end the curse. I tried but failed in Brooklyn. But now I was thinking - and it made sense after all - that the home had been here all along, and I alone - the very last one of us - could end the chain of suffering.

Optimism wasn't part of my nature, nor did my nurture inspire much hope, so I had my doubts about turning things around, especially after that cryptic warning from Mike about my brother. His personality dysfunction and bouts in prison aside, Sallie had been around this town his whole life, and he had to know some people even if he was the least friendly fucker these grounds had ever produced.

I finished early to go home and clean up before Mike arrived, but before doing so, I went across the street to the repair shop and gas station where Sallie had been working and staying before I baited him to Brooklyn and sent his ass back to prison, where he would soon meet his death.

The repair shop was right across the street from the Inn, at the town's main crossroads. It took up a whole corner with gas pumps out front welcoming cars from two directions on a half-circle drive. The main building was unique and historic with a storefront within a stucco, conical tower topped by a slate roof. A squat offshoot housed the cavernous garage where cars were repaired and maintained. I always admired the building and thought it too antique and too cool for a dirty garage and filling station.

The garage doors were open, and the warmth of the afternoon sun dissipated dramatically within the cool of the shaded repair shop, where my brother's old friend and boss, Huey Daniels, had an Audi Quattro elevated for an oil change.

"And how are you, Huey?" I said to his mammoth back and hunched shoulders.

He turned around slowly, looked at me askance for a moment, considering me like an apparition, his dark, dirty hair and beard flowing around the shoulders and collar of his overalls, just above where once formidable pecs were turning into tits. Like a lot of mechanics, he took on the appearance of his work environs. Everything smelled of oil and grease and exhaust, and it seemed to be absorbed by Huey. His white teeth behind his hairy smile seemed like a nice flash of humanity. He'd always liked me. Or so I thought.

"Heard you was back in town," he said, nodding approval. "Gonna yuppify that bar, they say."

"Who's they?"

Huey nodded towards the Audi. "Your friend the lawyer."

A kid I grew up with, Andy Alvino, worked in town as a lawyer; he'd helped me with some legal advice and represented me on the purchase of the Inn. The reality of living in a small town was becoming clear.

"I guess I'm not his only client," I said, nodding at the Audi.

"Shit," Huey coughed and gestured toward the shiny cars backed up outside the garage. "I'm under rides like this all day."

"So business is good."

"I guess, yeah, by normal standards," he said. "But the fucking landlord keeps jacking up the rent. Says now that the town's gone to money, he could rip out the pumps and turn this place into whatever he wants."

"Not a bar," I said, savoring the town's only liquor license and my ownership of the premises.

Hugh's half smile lasted about two seconds. We settled our eyes on each other.

"You hear about Sallie?" I asked.

"What about him?"

"He's dead."

Huey looked stunned for a moment, as he wiped his filthy hands on a filthy rag.

"I was wondering where he'd been," Huey said, trying to hide his shock under the guise of indifference that defined so many of us who grew up around men who mistook indifference for toughness.

It seemed smart for me to not say anything, to let Huey try to find some balance while revealing what he knew.

"He'd been working here, you know?"

I nodded.

"Making a fucking mess out of my office," he continued, with an uneasy chortle. "He'd been telling me that you two were working something out with your mother's house, how he'd be moving in there soon."

"And when was that?" I asked.

"Dunno. Three weeks, a month," Huey said, his head shaking from disbelief, throwing tools into a box just to do something with his hands. "Then one day, he was just fucking gone. I thought he found a broad or some shit. Maybe just hit the road for fuck's sake. Could never tell, not with that guy. Not like he was one to keep in touch. You know?"

"Yeah," I said. "Got that right."

Huey stopped banging tools into a metal box and started smacking a monkey wrench into his palm, looking at me square for the first time since the news of his friend's death had been delivered. Anger was settling in.

"The fuck happened?" he asked, a thread of suspicion in his voice.

"Don't know, really," I said. "Waiting on details, I guess, but he got himself thrown back in prison, and in there he came out on the wrong end of a knife fight."

"I don't believe it."

"He got jumped. Took one of them with him."

"That I believe," Huey said, a sense of relief bouncing around his face. He stopped pummeling his palm with the wrench. "There going to be a funeral or anything?"

"Hadn't thought of that."

Huey shrugged, knowing that Sallie wouldn't give a shit about anything as formal as a funeral. "I guess that's that," he said.

"I'll let you know if I find anything else out."

"Yeah, OK," he said, his chin lifted. "Thanks."

I was walking away, clothes glued to my body, when Huey called after me. He came out into the light and blinked away his blindness until ready to speak.

"There's a party at the AC a week from Friday," he said, a hand over his eyes like a visor. "You should come."

The AC was the Athletic Club, a ramshackle club house on the outskirts of town where members, only men, gathered to drink, shoot the breeze, and watch actual athletes on TV.

"What for?" I asked.

Huey looked at me incredulous. "To, you know, maybe talk to some of the guys about Sallie, a farewell of sorts."

When I was a kid, the AC was for upstanding men of town, men too dignified to drink at the Inn, on bar stools next to booze bags like my old man. The AC was for those with college degrees and stock portfolios and retirement accounts and the dignity of being self-made men who escaped the city and found success in the suburbs. Men with shins made shiny by slacks, who rode the train to work in Manhattan, reading the proper newspaper folded just right. I was aware that the Inn, despite its flaws, had become more respectable over the years, a place where the new money coming to town came to drink, and the good girls of my generation returned after college with their upstanding husbands. It made sense that the AC and the Inn had switched roles as the town increased in status, with the outliers now relegated to drinking and gathering on the fringes.

"Alright," I said, thinking that with Huey not knowing what happened to Sallie that I'd be in the clear. I'd be wrong about that.

. . . . .

I walked home in the first signs of dusk; the light fizzing on the horizon as birds took to the sky for a last go around before night sifted down. Cars passed stuffed with eyes popping at the long-haired stranger in town who walked everywhere. My preference for anonymity called for a haircut and a vehicle.

That being true, I was still filled with curious wonder about my hometown, about the years I had missed and any people who might remember me. I'd been a stranger everywhere I went for what was nearly half my life. The crossroads off the main strip led towards home, and I wondered as I walked past nice homes surrounded by tall trees how much of the population was new and how much had remained from my childhood; it was clear much had changed, a patina of new money, but still signs of a work in progress. It made sense. A town this close to the city with a fast train, schools, churches, a town pool, and a decent stock of houses. It wasn't so much the houses or the civic offerings or location that had burdened much of the town when I was young; it was the people who lived there. And my neighborhood was by far the worst of it, though it was still the '70s in America, when times were not good for a lot of folks.

I'd missed the '80s while out on the road, unaware really of our national identity, though I could sense the prosperity and nationalism, the mood that America was a special place, at least for some. I didn't feel much of that, out there on my own in the great, big world. I wondered where I'd fit in now that I was among the stable and the fortunate. I also worried about whether they would have me, or if I'd even want their welcome. Either way, I was ready to find out. Life had brought me here, without any other real option, so I'd find out if my fate was a blessing or a curse.

I entered our neighborhood as a train whistled past behind the houses on the high side, and the sky at dusk washed into an orange gloaming. I did as I'd been doing every day, naming names of kids who used to live in the houses I passed, kids like Brent Miller who routinely stole the mailman's truck and Keith Davids who broke windows with rocks and Teddy Parisi who came home with bloody knuckles courtesy of the nuns at the Catholic school and Frank Salerno whose dad had Penthouse magazines and Chuckie Driggs who lit fires and Drunkin' Joey Junkin who chugged Southern Comfort like water and Christopher Giordano who hopped trains all the way to Hoboken and Danny Doot who sold nickel bags of weed threaded with oregano and Jamie Convery who blew things up and Ike Van Hassel who did tricks with cigarettes and Skinny Vinny Giosa whose dad went out for ice cream one day and never came back. And their mothers in house dresses or waitress' uniforms smoking cigarettes on the stoop and the fathers who stuck around and collected trash and drove trucks and unclogged toilets and worked with iron and mowed manicured yards in other towns and unloaded ships all the way back on the docks in Brooklyn so they didn't have to live near minorities anymore. The kids were all gone, but I could feel them, and the nostalgia it inspired was almost too much to bear. It wasn't the type of childhood people wished for, but it was full of freedom and adventure and the type of challenges that, if you survived, could pay off in adulthood. That was my hope, at least.

Chapter 4

Mike picked me up at seven sharp, out of uniform in a Polo shirt, jeans and sneakers, but he still looked like a cop, all clipped and squared. He drove a pedestrian four-door Buick sedan, just like his old man. There was a cooler on the floorboards between the seats. Mike pulled out two bottles of Mexican beer and handed one to me. He twisted the top off of his and dropped the cap in the cooler. I did the same. We clinked bottles and drank in silence, parked in front of my house, at the dead end where so much of our childhood had been spent. This is where we met each day, since I wasn't welcome in his house and he was forbidden by his parents from coming into mine.

"Woo-ooh-oop!" Mike blurted, and I burst out laughing, spilling suds down my shirt.

It was the call he'd make, as kids, if he'd beat me outside. Sort of like ringing the doorbell without having to step on Stiles' property.

Mike, laughing too, clinked our bottles again, before putting his car in gear and driving the looping big block toward the neighborhood's exit.

"Can you believe this place?" he asked.

"Yeah," I said. "The trees really grew."

"Ttch," Mike chirped in his familiar way, when you missed his point. "I'm talking about the houses. You notice how much nicer they are?"

"No egg stains?"

"Yep."

Any kid or neighbor who fell out of favor, on any given day, could count on their house getting bombarded with eggs that night. And

Halloween was an all out egg war. But there were differences I'd noticed other than clean facades.

"You mean, like, how people park new cars in their driveways and not old cars to be fixed on the front lawn?" I added.

"There you go, Caes," he said with a grand nod.

"What happened to your house?"

"My parents sold it and moved to Florida."

"How are they?" I asked.

"Fine," he said, as if that would be a foregone conclusion, that they'd still be alive and doing well. His privilege of having two stable parents and sane siblings was always a problem between us, and a dozen years wouldn't change that, so I let it go, like always.

"Where we going anyway?" I asked.

"You'll see."

I sipped the beer, looked out the window as my hometown passed by, happy to go wherever my old friend took me.

.   .   .   .   .

We ended up at a tavern two towns over. We sat at the bar among all the familiar bric-a-brac of low-rent watering holes and ate overcooked cheeseburgers and greasy onion rings. Foghat played on the jukebox. Mike caught me up on all the kids we grew up with, and it wasn't pretty for the most part. Some had done all right, though. And as I had suspected, they were all long gone.

And then just as casually as asking if I wanted another beer, Mike asked what I'd been up to, so I told him how, on the day I ran away, I'd hopped a train to Pittsburgh where I lived under a bridge at first and eventually with two brothers from the Dominican Republic in a cold-water basement flat and worked as a line cook at a massive diner owned by a Korean immigrant whose niece I fell in love with and then got pregnant, which ran me out of Pittsburgh and led me to Iowa where I tended bar in a ramshackle joint for a depraved and violent man who caught me in a compromising position with his wife on a pool table, and the gun fight that followed chased me and her to an area outside of Denver where we holed up in a motor lodge and sold pills stolen from her old man until a private detective showed up to take her home and send me on my way, which was toward Austin, Texas, where I met a massive bluesman named Macie Turner who befriended me and took me on the road through the southwest, playing juke joints and road houses, where, outside Lafayette, Louisiana, I met a Creole child named Carmen with corkscrew hair and green apple eyes who taught me the local cuisine and how to Cajun Jitterbug, and how I would have liked to stay there forever with Carmen outside of Lafayette, until news from my mother about her illness brought me home, where I buried her alone, shuttered the house, and went to find a home in the mysteries of Brooklyn where all I really found was a missing art student on the dawn of gentrification and my vicious brother Sallie, out of prison early and needing to go back, so I set him up with the help of a Trinidadian vigilante, who was my friend, and a quasi-corrupt real estate developer, who was not my friend but paid twice what I'd invested only a year earlier in the two-family clapboard on a tree-lined block that I'd renovated beautifully, providing the profits to move back home and buy the Inn. And here we were.

"That's some story," Mike said.

I nodded.

"You should put it in a book."

"Maybe I will."

"You were always good at that."

"Good at what?"

"Telling stories, like your old man."

I shrugged. He continued.

"I thought about you when I was in the academy, out in LA, one of instructors talked a lot about police work being about details, noticing small shit that other people might miss, you know, overlook. And I thought about you and how you were always paying attention, noticing."

I could get behind that compliment, it might have been the nicest thing anyone's ever said about me. Beers were kicking in, and I was feeling good.

Mike signaled another round from the bartender named Jesse, a big, handsome woman with raven hair, a gap between her front teeth, "Mama Tried" tattooed on the underbelly of her forearm, and torpedo tits that tented the hem of her half-shirt. I liked how she kept out of earshot when not replacing our rounds, which she looked better with each time. She held my eye while placing our latest round on a coaster in front of me. I gave her a friendly nod and studied her swinging ass as she sauntered high and cocky like a house cat down to the far end of the bar where she resumed flicking through a magazine and pretended not to notice my interest.

Mike cleared his throat.

"Stay with me for a second, Caes," he said. "You're going to want to hear this."

"Go ahead," I said with one eye on Jesse.

"So, you were surprised to see Sallie out of jail so soon."

"I was, yeah."

"Did he mention how that happened?"

"Good behavior?"

"Heh!" Mike laughed his deep yelp when caught off guard by humor. "Good one, Caes. No, he ratted out a couple of his fellow inmates who were running a pharmaceutical operation with some guards."

"Ouch."

"Ouch is right."

"And I'm guessing they were pretty happy to see him come back so soon."

"Can you imagine?"

I decided not to think about it. The buxom bartender was of far more interest to me than the fate of my baleful brother. I'd been out of contact with the opposite sex for a while, and the single-mindedness of attraction, the deep longing in my chest and the humming of my loins, was coming on fast.

"So?"

Mike straightened up on his bar stool. "Well, besides the obvious, you might want to keep an eye out."

"For what?"

"The inmates that he ratted out weren't much to worry about, some half-assed white supremacy outfit that Sallie was apparently part of."

That didn't surprise me; Sallie was drawn to the hateful and the stupid. He also had absolutely no sense of loyalty to anyone or anything but his own raw instincts.

"But the guards who got busted," Mike continued with his eyes wide and serious. "They're apparently some dangerous motherfuckers."

"Whaddya mean?"

"Word is that these guys are part of a group that basically controls the prison, not to mention most of the vice in Hudson County. They got shit on everyone from the warden on down."

"And how do you know this?"

"Buddy of mine from LAPD who's now with the FBI out here."

"So what's this mean to me?"

"It means they might be looking for some form of reparations."

"What?"

"Reparations are kind of like..."

"I know what it means," I said.

Mike put his hands up.

"But what the fuck would that have to do with me? Hell, they should be thanking me for delivering his ass."

The inability to shed the stink of Sallie never failed to infuriate and haunt me; his reputation preceded me throughout my childhood, with teachers and parents and even the police. There were a lot of kids who were simply not allowed to hang out with me and girls forbidden from talking to me, teachers who despised me from day one. And, of course, I was on the radar of our half-assed local law enforcement squad who came by the neighborhood to harass us all on a regular basis and who confronted us whenever we left the neighborhood; it feels like half my childhood was spent running away from them, and that was largely due to the havoc Sallie reaped upon that town. They had it easy; they didn't have to live with him or with the consequences of his life.

Mike shook his head at my resistance. "Doesn't work like that, Caes. These are not normal people."

"Why doesn't somebody do something about them then?" I asked, pushing some of my resentment on to Mike. "Isn't that why we have law enforcement, to enforce laws?"

"That's what they had Sallie for," Mike said as his shoulders flared. "He was recruited as an informant by the FBI. I don't know how they pulled that off, but they did. All he had to do was lay low, stay out of trouble."

"Jesus Christ," I muttered. "Like that was gonna fucking happen."

I sipped some beer and thought of my imbecile brother as a federal witness. It made me sad for our country. Mike clapped me reassuringly on the back.

"There's no indication at this point that they'll come looking for you," he said with a mix of formality and nonchalance. "I just wanted you to know, and to, you know, recommend that you keep your head up."

"My head's always up," I said as I slipped off the bar stool and sought the bathroom. As I passed handsome Jesse, she lifted her face from the magazine and gave me a jangly smile.

When I came back, Mike was gone. I sat on my stool alone until Jesse sauntered over and pressed her palms into the bar top in front of me as her breasts launched like rocket ships.

"Your friend paid the tab and asked me to take you home," she said, her voice hoarse and heavy with playfulness.

"Did he now?"

"He did."

"Whose home?"

She laughed. "You choose."

I rubbed my chin as if in contemplation.

Chapter 5

Back at Jesse's apartment, the lower-level floor-through of a two-family, small Victorian home, we stripped off each other's clothes and fucked for a good while in her twin bed before falling asleep. She had soft sheets and firm pillows, and I dreamed, as I often did, of old lovers when with a new one.

Song was the 15-year-old "niece" of the Korean man everyone called "Uncle," who owned and operated the diner in Pittsburgh where I found my first taste of gainful employment on the road. Song arrived from Korea three months into my stint working in the kitchen at the diner. I spoke English with her, and she kissed me on a wind-whipped bridge, whisking away some of the pain I carried. I had more than a foot of height on her, so we made an incongruous couple standing up, but lying down, she fit on top of me like an appendage. The first time we had sex, on a blanket on the roof of the apartment building above the diner, where she lived, I came as fast as a flicked wrist, though I stayed hard enough to hold her on top of me as she keened and moaned and bobbed until another erection soon returned as I caressed her small breasts and watched luminescent clouds pass by the gibbous moon that slanted over her slender shoulders. The moonlight streaked her jet black hair with silver, and a curtain of moon glow draped her body like a veil.

We were both too young and stupid and hot for each other to think about birth control; we kept meeting on the roof until our relationship was abruptly put to an end. Song was sent away shortly after, and I was fired from the diner and encouraged to get the fuck out of Pittsburgh. I took the advice.

I woke in Jesse's bed with a hard on and a recurring curiosity about what became of Song. I imagined she got an abortion, went back to school and on to college and probably beyond, entering the world of academia or medicine or law, marrying a nice American from a good family. I hoped so, at least. It was best for her to split us up.

Jesse rolled over and bumped into my Song-inspired stiffy, so we took a slow, morning-tour of each other in the soft light filtering through thin curtains that billowed in and out of her open bedroom windows. I liked the earthen smell of women in the morning, and I preferred sex in daylight, so I was content on staying in Jesse's bed for as long as she'd have me, and as long as I could be of use, but her kitchen phone kept ringing, each time adding to her sense of unease. I got the picture. Someone was looking for her.

Too bad. I was thinking that we might be able to see each other again, but I'd been shot at already by a jealous lover in that ramshackle joint back in Iowa, and a gun had been inches from my face in Denver over the same affair, so I vowed then to stay out of other people's lovers. Jesse watched me dress with the sheet covers draped across her continental divide off a chest, her eyes pleading for me to stay and to go at the same time.

The sound of a bored-out, muscle engine rumbled down the street. Jessie's eyes blossomed like morning glories. I kissed her on the forehead and slipped out of the bedroom, through the living area and out the backdoor, where I crossed a small yard and deftly hopped a high, wooden fence and landed softly in the backyard of her neighbor as the portentous engine approached on crunching gravel then went silent in the driveway.

·   ·   ·   ·   ·

I walked home across two towns busy with morning hum. The sun had yet to rise above the trees; the air was cool and still and sweet-smelling. The road I followed led directly into town, so I bagged any thoughts of going home to freshen up. The deli down the block from the Inn had

Taylor ham, egg and cheese sandwiches and strong coffee. I took some of each around back of the Inn where two Latinos sat in the shade.

"And how are you?" I asked.

They scrambled up, both the same stocky size, black hair and eyes, thick hair shaved into tiny pins, deep brown skin, orphan clothes and duct-taped boots, eager, if not desperate, expressions. They were older than me but not by much. One of them handed over a crumpled piece of paper soggy with palm sweat.

C - here's the help you wanted. Thought you might be a little late so I told them to wait. They've been on the clock since 7:00. You're paying them $10 an hour. Hope you had a fun night. I'll swing by during the day if I can. Either way I'll get the Chicos at 5:00. Later. Mike.

Their bodies quickened but their liquid eyes stayed locked on mine, forthright, until I nodded toward the back door. I could feel the tension gust from their mouths and their shoulders relax as I worked keys in the metal door: Work. Pay. Security. That's what people want.

Inside was cool and dark. I led them through the corridor into the barroom that was empty except for natural light through windows stripped of cover. I motioned to the bar, where I put my brown-bag breakfast that couldn't contain the smell of salty ham. I held up a hand for them to stay. The front door was beyond a glass vestibule, and I went through to enter the street. Before I vanished, I made sure they were OK and staying put, with another assuring hand gesture.

I returned with two more breakfast sandwiches and coffees. We ate together standing at the bar. And then we got to work. By the time Mike arrived at 5:00, I had stripped and sanded the bar while my new guys, Santi and Jr., cousins from Ecuador, had filled the dumpster with crap out of the dining room and kitchen. They worked hard and knew how to use tools. I wanted as much of that old joint removed, so everything short of the foundation and the bar had to go. I needed to strip the stench out of the floorboards. We were going to tear it down and build it back up. This made the guys happy since they'd have work all summer. I liked the routine. And the company.

Chapter 6

A few weeks into the renovation routine with the cousins from Ecuador, on my way out alone after a long day, brimmed with contentment and a sense of progress, not to mention the benefits of physical exertion, I locked the back door and crossed the small expanse where we currently kept the dumpsters and where I planned to build the outdoor smoking section that Richie's demand required. A high hedge bordered the parking lot. The sky was soft and dark, and when I turned past the hedge a figure startled me from the shadows. It might have been the play of tricky light, but he appeared 7 feet tall. I stepped back toward the light above the exit.

"Working late this night?" a deep voice asked, pleasant enough but threaded with an accent that rang of menace and dark Europe.

I was in the light, thrown from the exposed bulb above the back door, and he was in the shadows of the hedge. I liked knives and kept one on me since the age of 12. I developed a real talent with blades as a runaway, mastering tricks and accuracy through endless hours of practice that an orphan has available while lost in America, but I'd also learned to use it to great effect when the undesirables came to prey on whom they assumed to be a vulnerable child. I'd cut people in remarkable fashion though my greatest feat was the ventilation of a game jersey on a degenerate linebacker from the state university in Iowa, a thorough display of virtuoso knife work that didn't draw a drop of blood but did receive a wild ovation from a crowded roadside bar, where I worked at the time as a bouncer and bartender.

ANDREW COTTO

The scenario with the man in the shadows seemed familiar, a threat that required violent response, so I slipped out my knife, pried open the long blade, and stepped into the darkness ready to draw some blood.

Moonlight escaped through thin cloud cover and reflected off the shiny and sharp blade. The large silhouette ensconced in dark stepped back and pulled up the collar of an overcoat. "Don't do that," his voice, calm and authoritative, instructed.

He was confident and foreboding, and this had no signs of a mugging, though he'd clearly been watching me without being noticed. I folded the knife and put it in my pocket.

"A man wants a word with you."

I was relieved in the moment by a purpose to the encounter, but daunted by its portent. I thought of Mike and his warning about Sallie and potential reparations.

"And what man is that?" I asked.

"Porter."

"Porter who?"

"Mr. Porter."

"The fuck is he?"

"You'll find out."

"Why would I do that?"

"Because if you don't this place will be a heap of ashes one morning, which would be too bad considering all of the work you have done."

It sounded like he actually meant those last words, though sentiment was not part of the scenario. He pulled his hand from the long coat and snapped; the phosphor of a match became a flame. He held it at shoulder height and his face looked erotic in the flickering light as he sucked the trail of smoke in through his nose. We had a few pyros around town growing up, and there was a sense of deviancy that they got from weaponizing fire and an indifference to the damage done. I was scared of people who liked fire. The flame had burned down to the large man's fingertips, and the smell of flesh entered the air.

"What's does this Mr. Porter want with me?"

"He will be the one who lets you know."

"And when will that be?"

"When you pay a visit to Glory Social in Bayonne." He snuffed the match in his mouth and flicked the pack at my feet. I picked it up. An address for Glory Social was handwritten on the inside. When I looked up, the giant, pyromaniac messenger walked slowly through the parking lot and disappeared into the darkness.

I went back inside and decided to sleep in the office upstairs and to purchase some fire extinguishers the next morning. I was shaken for sure, but also decided to keep this encounter to myself for the time being as to not interrupt the much needed stretch of peace and optimism currently in progress, as if I sensed its end looming.

ANDREW COTTO

Chapter 7

A week from that Friday, I cleaned up directly after work and waited out front for Huey to pick me up for the party at the Athletic Club. I sat on the curb, like I used to when I was little, waiting for kids to come out or hoping my father would come home. Coolness was settling through the canopy of trees, but I still felt hot and overdressed in steel-toed boots, jeans, and a black, cotton button down that gathered moisture on the shoulders from my still-wet hair. Out of habit and fear of a return from Mr. Porter's messenger, I brought my knife, though I kept it in my boot instead of my back pocket.

Cicadas chimed a riot, and their cacophony reminded me of summer evenings about this time when I was growing up and the neighborhood was filled with songs from the radio that blared from the car's worked on in the front yard next door, sausages were grilled, balls smacked off the curbs and sidewalks, and the cool of the evening settled like a veil on our skin still sticky from another long summer day. I always liked this time when late afternoon slipped into early evening; it held a promise of peace and whatever magic the night might bring.

Huey's roadster bogged into the neighborhood and took the swoop of the big block to the dead end. The top was down on the faded red MG, and his clean hair swept back off his ass-white forehead, showing more face than normal. He stopped in the middle of the street with his bullet of a ride pointed up the little block, "Funk 47" from the James Gang audible above the idling engine. I got in. Huey had on a faded Hawaiian shirt, long shorts and unlaced Chuck Taylors on bare feet. He nodded once I was seated and shot the car down the block.

I liked the wind in my hair and face. I waived to a few neighbors out in front of their homes. They waived back cautiously. It was odd to be the stranger on my old turf, but I didn't mind. There was newness backed by a sense of ownership. I'd triumphed and frolicked and suffered on those streets. We tore out of the neighborhood in Huey's convertible and through town, loud and fast, and it felt rebellious and maybe like the times I had missed as a teen with access to wheels.

I wanted to ask Huey who would be at the party, but the engine and the radio and the wind killed any conversation. Still, I pictured potential familiar faces and reunions and people happy to see me, though I wasn't sure of their names or faces. Huey cut the radio when we approached the AC, hidden by a cluster of trees on a road bordered by train tracks. The parking lot was nearly full with muscle cars and motorcycles and jalopies, and Huey crunched the gravel drive and found a spot in the far corner under the shadow and smell of mature pines.

My heart ticked around from the anticipation of entering a party. My head kept popping up though I tried to keep it down. The building was the color of bark and about the size of a double trailer under a metal roof pitched to both sides. An early AC/DC record played. A pig was being prepped for roasting over a makeshift pit, and burger smoke wafted from a charcoal grill. A cluster of men in their 30s and 40s stood around in small circles on the packed dirt, clutching beer bottles and talking in loud voices. Some dressed in shorts and t-shirts; some dressed like outlaws in leather vests with red bandanas around their heads. I felt overdressed and out of place. I didn't recognize anyone, and it occurred to me that, besides Huey, I didn't really know any of Sallie's old crew. They were five years older and never came around our house. Out of the house, I avoided Sallie as a matter of survival.

So, I felt fairly stupid approaching the party of strangers with Huey. A few guys with faces already mottled by alcohol came over, and Huey asked if any of them remembered Sallie Stiles' little brother. They said they did and shook my hand, but they were lying. I hoped.

A skinny guy in the crowd, with glycerin hair and leathery skin, walked away when he overheard Huey's introduction. His vest matched the others, and it read "Disciples" above some stitched flames: I wondered of what. Huey was recruited to help get the pig roast started, and I was left standing with a couple of the guys I'd just met. They told me to help myself to beers from any of the coolers scattered around, and to the burgers and dogs coming off the grill and stacked on picnic tables. It appeared, for the most part, a decent crowd of working class people, though there was an air of defeat among most of them.

I shot the shit the best I could, which isn't too good at all, and drank long neck Buds as the shadows stretched and merged with the darkness. Lights came on from inside the building and Bon Scott continued to growl over caustic guitar chords. I hot-boxed Marlboros and drank cold beer at a steady clip. Some older guys, two brothers who had grown up in town and had a house painting business, provided some decent company, especially after I took their business card for a quote on the interior of the bar when it was ready for painting.

The night wore on, and the crowd dwindled somewhat as the intensity of the party increased after the pig was carved up and doled out. Tequila and whiskey bottles and joints were passed. A record by The Who played. The language grew louder and more crude as party trash overflowed the garbage cans. People talked a lot about pussy, and I sensed meanness around the edges of the festivities. A disdain for women and successful men. Someone told a filthy, nonsensical joke about President Clinton's wife, and some wasted battering ram with his zipper down laughed his ass off and then asked out loud, "Who the fuck's Kinton?"

The skinny grease bag in the vest had left, but a few of his brethren remained. I caught them shooting sideways glances at me; at least, that's what I thought through the haze of booze and smoke. A couple of knuckleheads removed the head from the pig carcass and wore it around like a hat as brain matter dripped down their necks and onto their shoulders. Nice crowd.

A dented white van rolled into the parking lot and skidded to a stop. The side door slid open and that skinny fucker from before jumped out with three strippers in tow. The party roared and followed them into the Athletic Club where the interior resembled a furnished basement complete with a bar and sports memorabilia on the walls. I thought of cutting out and walking home, but Huey clasped my shoulder and ushered me inside. The music was deafening and the girls, white and trashy, danced around from man to man, priming the pump of desire. One of them, a concrete blonde in a spandex jump suit, took an immediate liking to me, much to the amusement of Huey and his cronies who cheered me on and left us alone on a leather couch in a corner by the door.

Her name was Marsha; she had fake tits and nubbed teeth and offensive perfume. She played with my hair and poured whiskey in my mouth. I didn't really like her company, but it was better than the rest of the crowd. When she shouted in my ear that we should go outside for some privacy, I accepted more for the promise of fresh air and quiet than anything else.

Outside was dark and cool, a respite from the smoke and noise and stench of a stag party. The moon cast pale light on the parking lot. Marsha took me by the hand toward a grove of pines in the dark shadows beyond the cars. Stars twinkled through the tree tops and crickets sang above the sound escaping from the club. Without a word or even a kiss, Marsha got down on her knees and went for my cock, which she did with impressive alacrity. Thanks to all the booze and dope, it took me half a minute to get hard in her mee-mawing mouth, but I reached erection status just as the first blow from a hard and heavy object landed on the back of my neck.

Marsha jumped away, and I fell where she'd been kneeling. The pain throbbing as a boot landed in my side and the object, which I made for a lead pipe or tire jack, landed on my back, and the beating began.

"Oh, my God. You're gonna frickin' kill him," Marsha screamed.

"Shut the fuck up," a man's voice said, and the pause allowed a glance through my raised arms. It was the skinny grease bag and two of his crew. Marsha ran inside as they resumed the beating that was clearly not arbitrary. The skinny guy with the tire iron kept saying, "That's what you get," though I was too busy protecting myself to do any thinking at the time. I knew how to take a beating, and I'd had much, much worse.

Besides the first couple blows, this was way more sound than fury and the work of individuals with limited capacity for damage.

The door to the club slammed open, and I heard Huey voicing outrage as he approached. When I untucked and sat up, Huey had the skinny fuck by the vest and nearly off the ground. I rolled over and fastened my pants, got myself standing as my head spun and the pain throbbed from damaged places around my body. Marsha chewed her fingernails and stepped on her own feet as others came outside. The two other assailants had drifted into the crowd.

"What the fuck, Funk?" Huey bellowed as he let him go with a hard shove.

And now I remembered him. Tommy Funk. A scumbag forever known for flushing a litter of kittens as a kid, a total fucking pariah and a hanger on to Sallie and his gang.

"That's what he gets for what he did to Sallie!"

I heard spit but didn't feel it land.

"The fuck you talking about?" Huey asked.

"He called me from prison, Sallie did," Funk said to Huey, his voice rising into a plea. "Said that his faggot little brother set him up in Brooklyn. Planted guns and drugs on him and then called the fucking pigs."

"That didn't happen," I said, even though that's exactly what happened. I wasn't too banged up to fight, and I was feeling the need for some payback and a change in conversation. I took a knee to access my boot and came back to standing with a six-inch blade at the ready.

Eyes went wide and Funk stepped back as Huey turned around to face me. I carried knives for their intimidation most of all. No one wants to bleed, and bleeding is a real possibility.

"Come on, now," Huey said with his hands up. "Take it easy, C."

I spun the blade quickly around my hand and moved around Huey, who stepped in front of me again. Everyone backed away, and Tommy Funk ran off like a fucking coward. I pinched the blade and pulled it back and took aim between his shoulder blades, but I let Tommy Funk run into the darkness; I'd have to catch up to him another time as I wasn't up for a potential murder rap or a foot race with a scared rabbit.

"Get a ride home?" I asked Huey, tucking the closed knife into my back pocket.

He looked at me hard, as if I'd asked him something far more complicated; and then he nodded and walked to his car as everyone else headed back inside to party. We didn't speak the whole way home.

Chapter 8

Mike heard what had happened at the AC, and he wasn't surprised. Said Tommy Funk had been in and out of the can his whole adult life, and that he and Sallie had run with the same supremacist outfit at Northern. Mike reminded me that Sallie's prison crew wasn't particularly formidable, proven by the inept beating they dropped on me, but the real danger was potentially in the cabal of guards Sallie had ratted out. I didn't tell him yet about the beckoning from Mr. Porter.

And it was with Mike's warning in mind that I remained vigilant throughout the summer as Santi, Jr., and I kept to our steady routine of renovation. They worked hard, and we made good progress despite the heat that settled on the sunken town most days. By late afternoon, we'd all be drenched and ready for Mike to show up out of uniform with a 12-pack of cold beer, which we would split four ways at a wobbly picnic table in the shadows of the parking lot out back.

I love that time of day, when the work is done and the shadows grow long; the slanted sunshine fuzzy and kind. Beer tastes so good in those moments, so refreshing and empowering, as if nothing could go wrong. And I always dreaded the last few sips of that third and final beer, when Mike would shake his can and the guys would tilt their last sips and put their empties on the table top, raise their worn bodies from the bench to gather their gear and climb into Mike's car for the trip two towns over where they lived together with their wives and children in a bungalow among a grove of birch trees by a bend in the Passaic River.

A sense of loneliness came over me when Mike and the guys left. I'd slow-drag on a cigarette and linger before locking up and heading out on foot in the sifting light, walking with the lightening bugs all the way home, where I'd drink wine and reheat the meals I prepared over the weekend, to keep busy when no one was around and there was little to do besides work on the house, read, smoke cigarettes, and wonder when I wouldn't feel so alone.

Loneliness haunted me ever since I hit the road. Even in times when I had steady company, even friendship and love, there was a lingering, empty feeling that's probably similar to someone who grows up underfed and can't shake that dread of hunger even when there's food to be had. The house wasn't helping. It felt abandoned, of old furniture and a layer of dust I couldn't remove. There were ghosts in every room, reminders of all the awful shit that went down within those walls.

Even sitting at the kitchen table, what's supposed to be a place of nourishment, caused unease since it was there that the small promise of my childhood ended and my life lurched toward the periphery of society, where the outsiders dwell.

I grew up tall and agile, engaged in steady delinquency and adventuring, but also a lot of sport. As unsupervised, practically feral youth, we had much time to kill after school, on weekends, and all summer long, so when we weren't hopping trains or throwing rocks or raising hell of some kind, we played games. My father, an amateur welterweight, taught us to box in the makeshift ring set up in the backyard; the town's grammar school was just beyond the gully that ran behind the back of my block, and we spent endless hours there, playing football on the grass and basketball on the courts. Street hockey happened on the dead end. But baseball was my favorite. I liked the focus required and the range of distinct skills. I'd also spent thousands of hours throwing a rubber ball against the back of the house or against the curb up front, waiting for the sound of a motorcycle engine to carry home my old man.

At school, I was always the first one picked at recess. And there was a pride in easily besting my better-off classmates, though I never once was a douche about it. I liked the kids in my class, and they liked me, though I knew why they never invited me over. One kid in particular, more of a sports fan than an athlete, even at a young age, recruited me for the Little League team his father coached, convincing his dad that my family's reputation unfairly extended to me, and that I was the best 12-year-old baseball player in town.

I rode my bike to their house on the other side of town, a split level with a basketball hoop in the driveway and an in-ground pool out back. The father, a lanky and kind man, smoked Pall Malls and watched me and his son have a catch in their front yard. I rode home with a white uniform with black and red stripes and the name and insignia of the local bank on the back.

I didn't tell anyone. Kept the uniform below my bed. I'd slip it on in secret and hustle to the ball field on my bike for magical games at twilight or on Saturdays. My friend's father, the coach, turned out to be one of the nicest men I ever met. He called me Willie Mays for the way I patrolled center field and collected any ball in the vicinity; when I pitched, he called me Tom Terrific after his hero, Tom Seaver of the New York Mets. I waited, almost breathlessly, for him to announce the lineup.

"Willie Mays will be in center field and in the cleanup spot; you guys before him just get on base, and he'll bring you home. Got it?"

And after the game, it was always flattery, especially one exchange that stuck with me for a long time.

"Willie Mays, you go six for six today or what?" he asked after we slaughtered the team sponsored by the town's supermarket.

I reminded him of the one ball that was caught by their center fielder.

"Right, right," he said, playing dumb. "But you know what? That was the best ball you hit all day. Kid didn't have to move. Just held up his glove. You know what they call that kind of contact?"

I didn't.

"A frozen rope. The most perfect ball you can hit. And you know who hits frozen ropes?"

I didn't.

"Hall of Famers hit frozen ropes," he said shaking my shoulder. "Hall of Famers."

That phrase became a mantra. Just the idea that I could be considered in the company of "Hall of Famers" made me feel special, possibly for the first time in my life. I wasn't even sure of what it meant, but I repeated it to myself all summer long, until my season ended at the kitchen table.

No one was home, and my uniform was getting filthy, so I washed it and dried it and put it on early. There was some lasagna in the fridge, among the meals my mother prepared and left for us before she went off to her waitress job, and I was huffing through a piece before leaving for my game. Sallie slipped in through the basement and appeared by the stairwell in the kitchen in a tank top and jeans, his big upper body ballooned by a fresh workout. He was breathing a little heavy and slicked by perspiration. A vein on his forehead bulged.

"The fuck is that?" he asked.

"Ma's lasagna."

"No," he huffed. "That."

"Baseball uniform."

Sallie huffed again and shook his head. "You know who plays team sports?"

"Pussies and faggots," I repeated, matter of fact, his common refrain.

"That's right," he said, annoyed that I had stepped on his line. "And that makes sense because you're the biggest pussy and faggot in this whole fucking town."

Sallie stepped up to where I sat, his stock torso casting shadows over me and my uniform. He stunk like a man's crotch. He was 17; I was 12. And I never knew why he hated me so much. I pushed back the chair to get up, and Sallie caught me under the rib cage with a left hook that knocked me and the chair into the corner. The pain was sharp and immediate. My head banged against the wall. Sallie laughed, pleased with himself, took my plate of lasagna and went upstairs. I held my side and caught my painful breath, hustled off to the game repeating "Hall of Famer" the whole way there.

At the ballpark, the pain intensified, but I kept it to myself. I was scheduled to pitch that day, so coach was calling me Tom Terrific and asking me to warm up. I told him I was good and hid my pain that was throbbing and radiating at my side. My mouth was dry, and I fought the urge to cough. Or puke. We were the home team, so I took the mound. It was hot and muggy, and I felt nauseous. My first warm-up pitch sailed over the catcher's head. I crumpled to the ground and began to cough out of control.

By the time coach reached me and sat me up, my chin and my neck and the front of my white uniform were splattered with blood. Above me was a circle of players from both teams and some parents behind them, peering down at the kid on the ground, all of them horrified by the site of me, stained as I was and aware of the awful knowledge that my Hall of Fame days were over.

Chapter 9

We had a soft opening at the Inn the weekend after Labor Day. The place looked great. Both sides of the split establishment, bar and restaurant, were accessed by separate glass doors on either side of the shared vestibule just off the corner of the town's main street at its primary crossroads. Perfect location. Both sides were long and narrow, but not too narrow, like parallel containers, and had clean lines and stained wainscot giving way to beige plaster, painted neatly by the two brothers I met at the AC party. No decorations on either side, only a faux-vintage jukebox nestled in the front corner by the bend in the bar and a tin ceiling spiked with wooden ceiling fans and exposed bulbs. We'd widened the windows that faced the street along the bar and put booths on that side, so people could stay in the bar to eat instead of going to the dining room that had circular four tops spread evenly over the refurbished floors. Frosted windows on the front side let in natural light but maintained privacy when eating, and similar ceiling fans with exposed bulbs turned the air and added light. I liked the continuity and minimalism. I favored less over more when it came to everything except sex and lost highways.

The two rooms met in the back, just outside the kitchen, in an open area where all the serving materials were neatly stacked in a makeshift staging station. The bathrooms, upgraded, shiny, and modern, were down the hallway from there, leading to the back exit where, just outside, the last aspect of the renovation had been completed: a metal-roofed, open-air portico that would function as a smoking section with

ANDREW COTTO

wooden benches, sand-filled buckets for ash trays, a wood-planked floor, and even a heating lamp for winter. It cost me a couple parking spots and the price of materials and a permit, but I'd take care of my smokers - as I was one of them - but I didn't want their pollution anywhere within my walls. The smoking ban was Richie's idea - a guy off the sticks for a decade who didn't need temptation in his face and lungs - but it also worked with my desire to keep the place somewhat family-oriented and as inclusive as possible.

The kitchen was the only part of the joint that didn't warrant a complete rehab. It was open and well-lit, in need of a few upgrades but otherwise functional. They'd left the non-permanent equipment, too, and I kept most of the pots and pans, the tools for opening, peeling, scrubbing, basting. I cleaned the vents and replaced the fryer and, of course, brought in new knives from a German craftsman I found in the Yellow Pages.

The menu came to me as I worked over the summer, got a sense of the town and its tastes, what was available locally and seasonally (Jersey is the Garden State, after all; there's also a lot of farms for meat, and lakes and coastline for fish). Of course, my own tastes were a factor as I wanted the customers to know a little something about the man behind the food. Not much of a talker, and often a stranger, cooking had been one of my main forms of communication as a young adult and even still. Now that I was back on somewhat familiar ground, I wanted the menu to reflect, in part, my identity, while recognizing at the same time this wasn't only about me.

.   .   .   .   .

At 5:00 p.m. sharp I unlocked the door and took a seat at the front corner of the bar by the refurbished jukebox. I picked a vintage Muddy Waters album and let the jaunty blues howl and bounce around the room as I took the time to reflect.

I sat there at the bar, eyes closed, one fist under an elbow on the bar; the other pressed against the lips of my bowed head, in the bright lights of a brand new bar, as if I knew something was coming, but I didn't know what it was.

39

The 5:15 whistle blew and broke my spell.

"And here we go," Richie said, strapping on his apron as I passed him on the way to the kitchen where I checked over my prep station for the 10th time. Santi was back there waiting by the dishwasher. I only had the need for one of the cousins, and I hired Santi over Jr. because he had some experience on a cooking line, and he was bigger and tougher, which might come in handy if Sallie's debtors came calling or if Tommy Funk and company bum rushed the joint.

"Ooohhh!" I heard Richie bellow from the barroom as people started filing in.

Within an hour I had to have Santi give up the dish washing to help me on the line. Orders came in steady from both the bar and the dining area. Lots of burgers, a few chops, and plenty of big salads. Staples, which I understood because it was opening night and people don't get adventurous until they're comfortable with the basics. I made the mistake of sending a couple of plates of lamb lollichops, single ribs quickly seared on both sides and eaten by hand, out to the bar to sample, and soon an avalanche of orders came in that cleared us out of the most delectable finger food on the planet. Or at least on my planet.

And while a slow night at a restaurant resembles time standing still in a certain section of hell, a busy night is light speed. Hours flew by, and I hadn't so much as thought about anything else but getting plates out the swinging doors and into the respective rooms.

"People asking for ya," Richie yelled into at the kitchen a few times while signaling orders that Santi would grab and post.

Santi proved to be skilled in the kitchen, and we were able to communicate through the common language of cuisine and good will. Things slowed down, food-wise, around nine, and I was able to take a smoke break after Santi and I tackled the stack of dishes.

The night was cool and still and bright; the new autumn moon, in a cloudless sky, shined like a porcelain plate high above the tree line. I stepped beyond the portico in place for smokers, to blow smoke at the moon and savor a successful opening. The relief was immense and optimism threaded through me, as if that something I felt coming was something good. I was eager to get back inside and maybe take a turn around the front room to see who was asking for me.

A handwritten note addressed to MY SON was duct taped to the back door. I took it down and unfolded the page. The note was written neatly and on the thick paper of the small journals my father used to keep full of poems or pictures or just anything that struck him to write down. It wouldn't have been unusual for him to stop in the middle of anything and yank the journal from his back pocket or the small of his back, tucked in the waistband of his jeans - and start thoughtfully scribbling in his practiced penmanship, his eyes unblinking and his hand moving carefully across the page. His formal syntax, especially in the written word, was contrary to the drunken belligerency that most associated with him, but I - more than anyone else - knew of him as a gentle and charming storyteller, a man of immense imagination and capacity for love, more poet than fighter to me. The most misunderstood of men. Sallie had run him off with a threat of death when I was 13, something I did not learn of until a year ago - when Sallie told it to me as a matter of spite - and I never stopped missing my father and remembering his stories and the touch of his hand on the top of my head.

In some ways my rebirth began with Sallie's confession since it preserved the image I had of my father as severely flawed but not the kind who would abandon his family in the familiar way. He and our mother were married but never really together, to my recollection, in a romantic sense as husband and wife beyond the making of three boys. I think they relied upon each other to escape the horrific environments of their tragic lives in the Bronx, of the deranged mother of my mother and the torturous orphanages of my father. My father slept on the couch on the nights he came home. The house belonged to my mother, and he made no bones about that or his plans of leaving once he saw to his boys growing up. He used to mention that he'd hop on his bike one day and take off for California, to live among the hills and hollows of the wine country or down near Mexico way in Baja. I had hoped to find him there one day. Instead, he had found me and would come out of the shadows when it suited him.

The large and looping cursive was still the same and a pulse of warm familiarity coursed through me, a breath I'd been holding for ages finally released.

My Son,

I see that you are well and that my faithful bartender remained true to his vow of silence. You may wonder why I don't walk into your barroom or knock on your door to say hello and have a chat, but my distance is best kept at this point. There's some things I need to explain to you about our family, but you have more pressing concerns at the moment. I've spotted a giant man I believe to be no less than 8 feet tall lurking behind your establishment on two occasions.

I ran him off with a curse learned from the witches who raised me, but I'm certain of his return.

I'll stand guard the best I can and save our reunion for another day.

Take good care, my son.

Your father, Timothy Stiles

Chapter 10

The next morning, I told Mike about the beckoning of Mr. Porter but not about my father's note. Mike chided me for not telling him earlier and called in late for work. We hopped in his sedan and scrambled south through the industrial byways of northern New Jersey, past the refineries that blight and choke the landscape spotted with marshland and the majesty of the Manhattan skyline shimmering on the horizon like a mirage. Planes from Newark Airport soared over the billowing smokestacks and silos and factories, past penitentiaries of concrete and barbed wire, through the ozone of natural gas and fecund swamp. It was the New Jersey stereotype writ large.

Mike entered Bayonne and navigated the downtown and residential grid as we worked our way toward the waterfront scaffolded with the apparatus for accommodating cargo ships. The colored containers were stacked like giant children's toys, and the cranes loomed like prehistoric predators.

"Been here before?" I asked Mike as he whipped the car around quiet streets dappled in morning sunshine.

"Where? Here? Bayonne?"

"No," I said. "Sacramento."

Mike laughed, though it was threaded with tension. Everything about him seemed tight, almost sticky. The ride had been silent, and I could feel him bristle like a transistor radio. I was a little preoccupied myself, not sure what this Mr. Porter wanted and not sure why Mike thought it was so imperative that we find out, but I was willing to trust Mike, if only for the exercise in trust.

"There's a gym near here," Mike said, after I'd given up on an answer. "Place you can spar with some tough motherfuckers."

"How'd you make out?"

"Not bad," he said, leaning forward to study the maritime edifices of the waterfront. "There it is."

Mike flipped down his sun visor and drove past a spacious joint jammed between two warehouses with Glory Social in neon in the barred windows beneath a battalion of flags that danced in the steady breeze.

"Where you going?" I asked.

"Around the corner."

"What for?"

"So not to be seen."

"You're not coming in?"

"Ain't me they're after," Mike said with a small smile, jerking the car across the divider lane and backing it into an alley before cutting the engine.

He looked at me like a coach or a boss, serious but encouraging. "If they ask how you got here, say you took the bus. Stop is just across from that park we passed a few blocks back - remember?"

"Yeah," I said, feeling suspicious. "And what exactly am I doing here again?"

"Came to see what this Mr. Porter wants with you, right?"

His tone changed to nonchalance, as if he was just dropping me off at the mall or some shit. Pricks zipped across my hairline and pores opened on the back of my neck. So much for exercises in trust.

"Fuck is going on?" I asked, suddenly displaced in the company of my oldest friend.

"Whaddya mean?" Mike chuckled in a manner that might have been convincing to someone who hadn't heard that disingenuous chuckle before.

"You know who this guy is," I said. "You know where we are."

Mike tucked his head into his chest and shook it back up with a contrite sigh. "It's not what you think, Caes," he said, looking me hard in the eye.

"I think when you found out about Sallie and all this shit with the guards, you're trying to do a solid by your buddy at the FBI for whatever reason, and you got me in the fucking middle of it."

Mike let his big laugh rip and punched the steering wheel with the side of his fist. "Jesus, Mary, and Joseph," he said, imitating his father. "You're in the wrong line of work."

"I'm in the business of staying alive," I said and immediately felt stupid for being self-righteous and using cliches and for thinking I had a right to be alive.

"Take it easy, now," he said, his face suddenly serious. "You're right. I've got my eye on getting the fuck out of Mayberry PD, but I didn't put you in this position. I'm helping you, guy."

"And why's that?"

"Because I'm your friend. You know that, right? How many times we help each other out growing up? Look out for each other. Right?"

I studied some seagulls perched on the eaves of a row house across the street. I wished my mother was still alive. Mike smacked me on the shoulder with the back of his hand.

"Couple of weeks ago, I had to respond to a call over on Rodney Street, behind the school. Some lady was in a panic cause there was a squirrel, and I'm not making this shit up, there was a squirrel in her backyard with what she said, and I quote, 'an unidentified object' in its mouth."

I looked at Mike.

"You believe that shit?" he asked. "This is what I'm faced with here, and I can't take it anymore. My mind is turning to mush. Out in LA, I was in some serious shit, life and death everyday with the gangs in Ramparts or South Central, and I couldn't take any more of that either. It was like working in a war zone. The stress was crushing me. So, no can do on that, either. I'm looking for a steady law enforcement job, nothing too crazy and nothing too boring. Real investigating, with maybe a little rough stuff on the side. The Feds would be perfect, so, yeah, excuse me if I see this as an opportunity, but it's not one I, you know, manipulated or anything. It's about being here for you, first and foremost. Unless you don't want my help. We can go home right now, but this Mr. Porter business will not go away on its own. That I can tell you."

I tried to make sense of things by staring at the seagulls again. The sun bounced off the windows of the shabby row houses. Big rigs rolled to and from the docks. A brackish smell from the water beckoned the birds off their perch and they extended their alabaster bodies into flight that freckled the blue sky. I thought of finishing this business with Mr. Porter and finding out what my father had to tell me.

"What was it?" I asked Mike.

"What was what?"

"The unidentified object of the squirrel."

"Never found out," Mike said with a solemn shake of his head, his lips flattened to fight off the smile. "Never found out."

I walked out of the car and headed for Glory Social.

Chapter 11

The small parking lot in front of Glory Social was dotted with American cars and pickups, except for a red BMW by the door in a spot reserved for "Da Boss." The facade, stabbed with flags, was faded and resembled more of a rec hall than a watering hole. A sign by the door read "Members Only"- and I walked in to find a squat man in a beach chair doing a late Elvis impersonation with a jet black pompadour and matching mutton chops. Some of the hair dye stained the top of his ears. His dress shirt, open to the solar plexus, showed a gold medallion, serious cleavage, and no hair. His girth pushed on the waistline of his slacks. He stood up and his stomach lunged in my direction as he pulled off dark sunglasses and smiled without showing any teeth.

"Wrong door," he said, looking up at me as wrinkles bloomed around his squinted eyes. "Members only."

The room was bigger than it appeared from the outside, of exposed brick with windows in back that overlooked the water and welcomed bands of sunlight that illuminated a swarm of dust motes and covered two pool tables, one of which was being used by a trio of dock workers playing cut throat. The cracking balls filled the empty room with its only sound. A gaggle of other waterfront creatures lounged at the bar that ran along the far wall where a tender with a monstrous head, wide shoulders and tremendous height polished a pint glass with a bar rag and held my stare until a thick finger poked me too hard in the chest.

"Deaf?" Fat Elvis stood and asked me. "Or after a beatin'?"

He shifted his weight easily into a defensive stance and expanded through his shoulders. My chest still thumped from his poke.

"And how are you?" I asked him.

"Not friendly," he said.

"You don't say," I replied.

"But I do," he shot back, a tilt to his head indicating, perhaps, that he was enjoying our exchange, though I knew my window for witty banter was small and shrinking.

"A Mr. Porter asked for me."

"Says who?"

"Says him," I said, looking for the bartender, who was nowhere in sight.

Fat Elvis glanced at the bar then back at me. "One of two things is going happen in the next 30 seconds. One, is that a man, very handsome black guy, is gonna come through the door there behind the bar and call you over. Two, is that I'm gonna escort you with great prejudice out the front door and maybe as far as the next block."

I nodded and waited for Fat Elvis to make his move before driving the steel toe of my boot into his kneecap and then booking it back to Mike's car. The irreverent and dangerous doorman crossed his arms over his barrel chest and positioned himself between me and the barroom. From over his head, I kept an eye on the door behind the bar and watched the top of the pompadour for movement. I counted my breaths in steady rhythm, letting just enough adrenaline slither through my body. The room smelled of stale smoke and beer-soaked floors. At 29 breaths, the pompadour jerked and I grabbed at his neck with my left hand to steady for a strike with my right foot, but before I could deliver, a door slammed. I released the shirt collar; the necklace and medallion fell to the floor.

Fat Elvis had a thick vein bulging at his temple and his nostrils flared. His eyes looked like they were about to escape the sockets.

"Sorry about that," I said as I walked past him toward the man who waited for me at the marble bar fronted with a shiny mahogany lip. I immediately knew to whom the red BMW belonged.

Mr. Porter was a fit, natty man with fledgling white patches on his black face and hands. I'd seen that condition before but never knew what it was called, and it always struck me as particularly unfortunate, even ironic in a cruel way, for a black person to sacrifice an aspect of appearance and identity to an ugly whiteness.

"And how are you?" I asked, extending my hand as I approached the bar.

Mr. Porter smiled, impressed, I assumed, that I was neither scared nor anti-social, though I was both. I knew his type: serious men of great intelligence and danger. The type of men who'd have been emperors or generals in different times, maybe titans of business or politics or law today if life had afforded such opportunities, but who instead operated with great success beyond the periphery of modern society. I tended to like his type, being a fan of confident, self-made people and preferring those out of the American mainstream.

Mr. Porter's hand was heavy and smooth; his eyes twinkling blue matched the pressed dress shirt open at the collar.

"Have a seat," he said with a brassy baritone. "Offer you a drink?"

"Sure," I said, not wanting a drink but happy for the chance to calm my nerves after the near throw down with Fat Elvis, who appeared in the bar mirror holding his busted jewelry and staring a dagger into my back.

"Let it go, Ant," Mr. Porter called to him. "I'll take care of it."

"I got this down in DR," he said.

"We'll go back," Mr. Porter assured him.

Fat Elvis agreed with a smirk and a nod put the broken gold in his pocket and resumed his seat by the door. Mr. Porter smiled at me and nodded over my shoulder.

"Some character, huh?"

"I'll say."

"Did a 20-year bid before getting out and finding gainful employment with me."

"Looks like the right man for the job."

"Think you could've taken him?"

"Probably not," I confessed.

"What was the plan?"

"Take out a knee cap, make for the door."

Mr. Porter nodded, pinched his mouth, then rested a finger on his chin.

"See if you could make it to your friend's car before we caught up to ya?"

I didn't ask how he knew about Mike around the corner, something Mr. Porter seemed to appreciate.

"About that drink," he said.

"Manhattan."

"Bourbon or Rye?"

"Rye."

"My man," Mr. Porter said.

He worked the bar with alacrity, and had the amber cocktail produced in half a minute, orange peel garnish (no cherries), in a heavy, low-ball glass.

"Thanks," I said and took a sip. "I should come here more often."

The smile about split Mr. Porter's face in two. And then it disappeared.

"Your brother caused me a lot of problems," he said.

A coughing/laughing fit of which I'd never known erupted from my chest and garbled out my mouth like ocean water. I leaned over the bar, clapped my chest and bumped the marble slab with the flat of my fist.

Mr. Porter waited patiently, amused.

"Sorry. Sorry," I said after regaining a semblance of composure. I took a big sip of my drink to wash down the fit inspired by the absurdity of Mr. Porter's statement.

"I gather you two weren't close."

I held up a hand to please make him stop.

"Understood," he said, "but regardless of that, your brother - and a couple of cohorts - put me and my operation at the penitentiary in great jeopardy."

I still had some lingering jangle in my chest that I washed down with the last of my cocktail.

"And it's incumbent upon me to make sure that said threat is entirely eradicated."

Mr. Porter sounded like the lawyer or politician he could have been in another life.

"Seems pretty eradicated to me," I said.

Mr. Porter huffed, smirked, then reset his face. "For the most part, yeah, but I'm still after a few loose ends."

I sat silent. Mr. Porter pointed at my glass. Day drinking is something I try to avoid, as it can be very appealing, and I was also aware that Mr. Porter there might be after the "veritas" or truth that comes with libation, but - damn - that first drink tasted good, and I wanted another. Maybe even needed one.

"Thanks," I said and went back to silence as Mr. Porter removed my glass and fixed a new drink in a fresh low ball.

"You are aware that your brother was cooperating with federal authorities?" He asked with the placement of the Manhattan in front of me.

"Nope," I lied. "And thank you."

The sound of pool balls had stopped and there was no one in the mirror behind me except Fat Elvis who had begun work on a size stogie.

"Where'd everybody go?" I asked.

"Out to lunch."

"That front door locked?"

"Maybe."

"What did Sallie have on you?"

Mr. Porter laughed. "Sallie? He went by Salvatore on the inside."

"Can you blame him?"

"Nah."

"So, what did Salvatore have on you?"

"That's what I'm asking you."

I took a nice sip of the Manhattan and looked Mr. Porter in the eye in order to deliver some of that veritas he was after.

"Listen," I said. "The person you know as my brother was not my brother. We had the same parents, grew up in the same house, shared a brother even, but were not of any relation. In fact, I hated him. And he hated me more. I'm glad he's dead, and I'm glad he's gone."

"That's some cold-blooded shit right there," Mr. Porter said. "But you don't strike me as being particularly cold-blooded. Smart. Yeah. Smooth as a motherfucker, too. I'll give you that, but I'm not feeling the cold-blooded coming out of you."

"Want me to open a vein?"

"I want you to tell me something that will make me believe what you're telling me."

I checked the mirror to make sure Fat Elvis hadn't moved.

"You know how Sallie ended up back in prison?"

"Heard he got picked up in Brooklyn on a weapons charge."

"He was blackmailing me for our mother's house, something I needed very badly to keep, so I set him up, with the gun and some drugs, too, baited him into the violence that brought the heat. I even had the cops waiting there when it happened. Check with the arresting officers, off the record, if you want."

"Mios fucking dios," he said, with the first hint of Spanish accent detected. "So you are cold-blooded."

"Only when I have to be."

"You know of anyone your brother might have told about his cooperation? About any evidence or pending testimony he might have shared?"

I buttoned my lips and shook my head.

"He made a call from prison. Do you know to whom?"

"A lawyer?"

Mr. Porter nodded. "You would think, but he didn't, which has me thinking the call was to somebody who has information I might want."

"Why do you think that?"

"Because your brother tried his blackmail practices on me, as well."

"You don't say."

"I do, and I don't believe he was acting alone."

"I don't want to undermine your suspicions, Mr. Porter, but Sallie was not exactly a people person."

"That may be so, but he did have a crew in prison, like anyone who wants to stay alive, and he apparently had some connects on the outside as well."

"How do you know?"

"Let's just say the blackmail didn't die with your brother, and I'm thinking it's that person he called from prison."

I had a hard time imagining Tommy Funk in the blackmail business, up against the likes of Mr. Porter.

"You know any of your brother's connections?"

"I'd been gone for 12 years," I said. "Practically a stranger in that town."

"Who's outside waiting for you in the car?"

"He still there?"

Mr. Porter looked up, and Fat Elvis, with his back turned, held up a pointer finger. Mr. Porter nodded and waited for an answer.

"Just a ride," I said. "I don't drive."

Mr. Porter smiled and wrinkled a curious brow. "Said you'd be gone 12 years?"

"Yep."

"Where to?"

"Lots of places."

"I'd like to hear this story."

I finished off my drink and backed off the bar stool. "I'll let you know when I write the book."

"Do that," he said with a nod toward the door.

I nodded back and made for Fat Elvis, fighting the imbalance of nerves, massive relief, and two stiff drinks for lunch. His cigar smoke smelled good.

"And let me know if you hear anything else that may be of interest," Mr. Porter called to my back. "Be worth your while."

I held up a hand and swayed clear of Fat Elvis as I passed. "Catch you later," he said like we were old friends, expecting to see each other again.

Chapter 12

Mike pulled up in front of my house after non-stop questions halfway home, followed by silence for the rest of the ride. I hated to disappoint and also to deceive, but I had no sense of how any of the information Mr. Porter shared with me could be of benefit to Mike and his pal in the FBI. Keeping Mike away from Mr. Porter and company seemed like the best play. I was more inclined to help Mr. Porter, but instinct told me to keep what I knew to myself.

Tommy Funk would pay soon enough, with or without my input, a matter of natural selection in the criminal world. Another human stain removed from the planet, and that didn't bother me at all. Maybe I was cold-blooded, but I'd come to believe that not all lives are sacred and the world could use a few less fuckheads.

As I reached for the door handle, Mike put a hand on my forearm.

"And nothing else, right?" he asked. "Nothing that could be taken for extortion or reparations or obligation?"

"Nope," I said, eager to get out of the car. "Just tying up a loose end."

"All that time in there tying up a loose end, huh?" he asked with a jangly smile. "I was shitting my pants out there."

"You mentioned that," I said and Mike looked away. "Oh, by the way, they made you, right off."

"They did? Fuck. How'd you know?"

"He told me."

"Who did, Porter?"

"Yeah."

"Wha'd you tell him?"

"That you were my ride," I said as I got out, but leaned back in before closing the door. "And thanks for that, for the ride. Appreciate it."

"Sure," Mike said with an honest smile as his eyes lit up. "You by chance get a load of Mr. Porter's first name?"

I shook my head.

"It's Cha Cha," Mike said, nodding with a big, wobbly smile. "You believe that shit? Cha Cha!"

"Dominican?" I asked.

"Yeah," Mike said. "Mix. Black and Dominican, out of Mattison, actually."

Mattison was the small, nearby, impoverished city where mostly blacks and Latins lived; we weren't supposed to go there as kids, but we did anyway to score dime bags of weed and six packs at bodegas. A lot of kids lost their virginity in the Latin whore houses. I got knocked off my bike there once and beaten pretty good. My father worked, on and off, in one of the textile factories along the river, and he used to take me there on occasion on the back of his motorcycle to stare at the magnificent waterfall in the center of town. We'd sit there for hours just watching and listening to the water plummet into the deep and rutted gorge.

I offered Mike dinner at the Inn, slammed his door and went inside, hoping for a rest before work but unable to stop thinking about Mattison and Cha Cha Porter and the sense that our business wasn't finished. And that it had a connection to other matters in motion.

Chapter 13

The house was small and dark. I couldn't get myself to redecorate or even improve the interior appearance. It was just like my mother left it, same furniture and appliances and carpets. Candles and ashtrays. Faded paintings of southern Italy. A Ray Charles record on the turntable. Stiff sheets on the bed. The kitchen was small and had a shitty stove and worn linoleum tiles that curled in the corners. The walls were avocado from some awful '70s fad.

I started to take my meals out of the house, at delis and diners that New Jersey had plenty of, and I cooked for myself at the Inn once the kitchen was operational. I just couldn't get comfortable there at home. I slept in the den where my mother died, and often sat on the curb out front where I used to wait for my father to come home.

The neighbors thought I had rocks in my head, and I didn't get much interaction beyond obligatory waves. I really only had two neighbors, posited where I was near the dead end. The house on the end, once home to a derelict brood, was abandoned, still scarred from a house fire that happened shortly after I'd run away (my mother had told me in one of her letters that the oldest brother fell asleep, stone drunk, with a lit cigarette). At least there were no more cars parked on the yard, though the listing above-ground pool was a blight. Across the street was a small house of a childless, elderly couple who called the cops on us as kids on a regular basis. The blinds were permanently drawn, and I only saw the husband, well into his 80s now, slowly picking up his daily newspaper off the driveway. Right next door was a polished and manicured version of what the neighborhood had mostly become: a shiny couple with one toddler and two cars, an in-ground pool in back with a high fence for privacy. Her name was Sarah and he went by Steven, and they were nice enough but never asked me over to any of the steady barbecues they threw over the summer.

The Inn was starting to feel like my home, and I'd even stay a few late nights in the space upstairs, an open flat above the barroom with a low ceiling and windows on two sides. It had a shower and a leather couch, antique desk, lamps, and file cabinets left by the previous tenant, a lawyer from town who had merged his business with another right before I bought the place.

My clothes started migrating from the house to the flat, and I filled up the bathroom with toiletries. Part of it was my affinity for such spaces, and part of it was simply the convenience of not having to walk back and forth from home to the Inn. Mostly, though, it was clear to me that the house I grew up in would never be my home. It was impossible for me to escape the noise that still bounced around its walls, the trauma that filled the spaces. Every room housed bad memories. We had failed there as a family, and that couldn't be redeemed by me and a paint brush and new furniture from Huffman Koos. It was just as broken as that house next door with the listing pool and the fire-scarred facade.

That writer who claimed you could never go home again was dead right. And he was talking about regular homes. Imagine if he'd had a load of mine? It wasn't always awful, other than Sallie. My father had his stretches of sobriety when he could be charming and informative. My mother was an angel; my brother Angie a prince. I felt their love and knew what it was, so I would not give up on redemption for me and my family, and the promise I'd made to my mother before she died to find a home and end our family's curse. Even if our old house was not the home involved. I'd have to keep looking.

Chapter 14

The day I met Cha Cha Porter was the same night Dinny Tuite and I had our only exchange at the Inn. Dinny had been gone about 30 seconds, and I was still thinking about Richie's casual racism and trying to unpack what else was bothering me about Dinny Tuite when the bartender cleared his throat.

"Funny how old Dinny there sat right in that very same spot where your father was all those years," Richie observed with a whimsical look on his hard, Irish face.

There it was. Dinny Tuite reminded me in some ways of my father, that coiled aloofness and a sense of displacement. Layers and layers of complication belied by aspects of tremendous appeal. Some underlying currency that pulled you in if you were the rare type to recognize it.

I imagined my father in that very spot - 7 or 8 beers in, a whiskey on the side - unwashed hair and a sleeveless leather vest, duct taped boots, drinking the daylights out of a perfectly fine afternoon, holding court as his cigarette burned into the bar top and Richie quietly let him know it'd be time to go home soon, where - unbeknownst to either of them - his youngest son waited on the curb for the sound of a motorcycle and the return of his father. I so didn't want the Inn to be that kind of place anymore - where men hid from their families - and it had clearly been changing along with the town before I came back and fixed the place up, but I still had a public mission, and a personal agenda. I stopped thinking about Dinny Tuite, who was nothing more than a minor curiosity at the time, and started thinking hard about my father.

"He hasn't been in since that time..." It was a muddled question without any real context, but Richie knew what I was talking about.

"Who? Your father? Nah. Hadn't seen him since."

I was glad Richie lied to me about his communications with my father. He was keeping tabs and keeping a promise. The reality was that Richie had already told me enough about my father, the first time I met him, and we wouldn't be where we were at that moment if he hadn't.

I got the idea to buy the Inn during a visit from Brooklyn the previous year. There was some business with my mother's house, with the lawyer upstairs, and I stopped in for a pop, to take a look at the place my father had spent most of my childhood. Richie recognized me, pegged me for the son of Tim Stiles, which threw me for a serious fucking loop as I'd been in anonymity since leaving town more than a decade earlier, and I hadn't realized that I'd grown into a semblance of my old man whom I hadn't laid eyes on or heard a word from since he abandoned us when I was 13.

And then Richie sent me nearly out of my mind when he asked if I was meeting my father there, as he stops in from time to time. I figured the man for dead or at least long gone. And it was in that dazzling moment I decided - if I survived my looming encounter with Sallie - that I'd sell the Brooklyn duplex I had renovated and move back home, buy the Inn and fix it up, and wait for my father to stop in some time. I had other things to consider, as well, but I had that hope tucked like a feather in the cap of my heart as I prepared all summer long for reopening the Inn.

. . . . .

The 5:30 whistle blew and people started coming in the barroom. I took Richie's plate to the kitchen and continued to prep for dinner, working first on the steak sandwich Mike would have when he arrived for his pre-night shift meal. I encouraged him to try other things, but he insisted on the steak sandwich, said it was the best thing he'd ever tasted. It broke my heart when he put ketchup on it, but I forgave him and his tragic Irish palate.

59

Later that night, with a napkin tucked into his collar to keep his uniform clean, Mike told me all about Dinny Tuite being a pariah in the town, how Katie Donaghy, one of the middle sisters and closest to our age, had met him at Fordham, where he was on a track scholarship, and brought him home for suburban domestic bliss. He worked on Wall Street at a boutique firm as a trader and had a reputation for being aggressive if not risky with trading but had done really well for himself despite it all.

"And how do you know all this?" I asked him.

Mike's big brother Rob was a hot shot Wall Street guy, which didn't surprise me since he was ambitious and hard working even as a kid, avoiding all the neighborhood chaos for newspaper routes and lawn cutting jobs and life guarding at the town pool. Mike had consulted his brother about Dinny Tuite's professional life after troubling rumors emerged about him and one of the town's favorite daughters.

According to the townsfolk, Dinny Tuite was unfaithful and violent; he often drank too much and started fights at friendly small town gatherings; he had the esteemed Donaghy family in the midst of civil war due to all the dirty laundry flowing from the home of one of their perfect familial prodigies.

Mike had dated Katie Donaghy in high school, and he was close with the family. Even Mr. Donaghy - a hard-nosed, no-nonsense life insurance broker out of the old Irish ramparts on the northern tip of Manhattan - had come to Mike with his beef.

Even with all the sentiment stacked against him, and my own somewhat acrimonious encounter with the man, there was something about Dinny Tuite that had me on his side. We might not have been compatible, but we were from the same tribe.

Chapter 15

I called on Huey one afternoon. I hadn't seen him around, and his garage had been closed more than open as of late. It was raining, cold and sideways, a little fog setting over the sunken town along with the early shade of shorter days in middle October. I'd been working on trays of meatloaf all afternoon, and a poached garlic sauce to ladle on top. I covered a piece, minus the sauce, on a plate with tin foil, tilted up the collar of my jean jacket, and tucked a shoulder into the wind as I crossed the street through the headlights of passing cars.

"And how are you, Huey?" I asked entering into the shelter of his open garage.

"Oh, hey, C," he said, turning from his work under an elevated Chevy, a light hanging from the axel.

Huey looked worn and frumpier than usual.

"You all-right?" I asked. "Haven't seen you around."

"Yeah, well," he said, scratching some neck beneath his greasy coverall, "been taking some time off."

"Brought you some meatloaf," I said.

"Thanks," he said, and motioned his head toward a steel cart where I balanced the plate on top of some wrenches.

"You could come eat anytime, you know," I said with a shrug toward the Inn. "On me."

"Thanks," he said, though I knew I'd never see him. The Inn, even before I bought it and fixed her up, was a symbol of a change that didn't include the likes of greasy Huey Daniels. He had that hang-dog, defeated countenance, like my father when he was out of work or on the booze or in his black dog days.

Huey and I looked at each other for a moment, unsure of what else to say when the door to the office opened and through it stepped Tommy Funk.

"Now hold on a second," Huey said, but Tommy Funk bolted out the open garage before the sentence finished.

I was after him in an instant, one of Huey's larger wrenches clutched in my right hand. Funk took the corner away from the Inn and bolted up the town's main road. The rain lashed at my face and dampened my hair as I stomped my boots on Funk's trail. I peeled off my jean jacket without slowing down and left it on the sidewalk in front of the Five & Dime. Pedestrians jumped out of the way and surely had never seen such a pursuit through the business section of their quiet town. Two long-haired freaks, looking like they fell out of 1979, chasing past the storefronts lit up for business before supper time on a rainy, autumn weeknight in a quaint commuter town.

The warning bells by the tracks went off and the wooden gates came down.

The road inclined toward the tracks, and I gained on Tommy Funk as the exertion took a toll on his slight body compromised by Marlboro cigarettes and other bad habits. I could hear myself breathing hard too - a smoker myself, but a moderate one and the taker of regular exercise and good eating habits - careful to dodge the pedestrians whose innocent paths we crossed. They seemed to be popping out from between cars and out of storefronts like a video game, slowing my pursuit, though I was able to angle around them all until the commercial stretch ended and I was 20 yards behind Tommy Funk with the tracks just ahead.

A train whistle blew, and a locomotive barreled through trailed by a chain of industrial freighters rattling the eastbound tracks toward the city. The freight cars were forest green, almost black in the dreary light, red warning markers evident on each oblong berth.

ANDREW COTTO

My jeans were now stuck to my legs and lifting them became an effort, my t-shirt stuck to my skin; my lungs burned, but I focused on my breath that pumped from my chest in vaporous plumes and held tight to the thought of putting the fear of god into that motherfucker who had the balls to attack me from behind in the middle of a bad blow job.

A voice in the back of my head urged me to stop, to let it go for now, to remember that Cha Cha Porter would catch up to Tommy Funk soon anyway, and maybe I'd help that along, but the sight of that fuckhead set me off, and I was more offended by that surprise beating outside the AC than I had recognized. I was also more drawn to violence than I liked to admit.

Tommy Funk turned down the near tracks and ran next to the freighter along the open railroad ties. I cut that way but stayed on the sidewalk that led to the platform where a few people waited under the metal overhang for commuters from the city. A little boy held his mother's hand. On better surface, and in better shape, I gained quickly on Tommy Funk and was almost even when I reached the platform and the freighters, out ahead, pulled away toward the bend in the distance.

"Heads up," I yelled to the backs that were facing the city, waiting for the whistle. As they turned they saw Tommy Funk run past and then me, hot on his heels, burning past to the end of the platform when another whistle blew in the distance and I jumped off the platform onto the back of Tommy Funk.

We thudded down together, and I used as much of his skinny body as I could to break my fall with extreme prejudice. He made a moan of some sort, of fatigue and anguish that gusted out of him like a last breath. Someone screamed as I turned Tommy Funk over and reared back the wrench, the pain flashing across my chest and my knees that bore into the large gravel rocks between the tracks and the ties. All was silent for a lovely moment until a train whistle blew in a frantic staccato joined by a mechanical and metallic screech, and then a collision of immense force. The first sounds were of impact and twisting metal, but I ignored it.

63

Tommy Funk covered his face as the wrench landed across his forearms and an explosion erupted in the distance. I looked down the tracks, and a ball of flame rose through the mist and above the trees beyond the bend. I could smell the gas immediately as it blossomed into flame and then evaporated into dark clouds. The people on the platform gasped. There was silence for a frozen moment as black and blue smoke billowed, and panic ensued.

Chapter 16

I ground Tommy Funk's face into the gravel as I climbed off of him. He scurried away and lurched off as observers hesitantly made down the tracks towards the explosion. The rain lashed at my back and wind fingered my wet hair. My breath came deep and steady as I turned and walked away, against the current of bystanders and first responders. Sirens whirled and spun colors that reminded me of the markings on the side of the dark freighters. It must have collided with the 5:15 on that dangerous bend I knew all too well.

My brother Angie had died there. The seminal event of my childhood and what had sent me away from home all those years ago. I was not walking down towards that bend in the tracks where my worst memories and regular nightmares lived in a hollow that I'd never escape. Down the sidewalk, I felt like a river fish going the wrong way as the townspeople came out of their cars and the shops to investigate what was happening by the tracks. They brushed my shoulders in their haste, but I kept my eyes straight ahead and tried not to run back to the shelter of the Inn as sirens wailed from various directions.

I picked up my jean jacket from the sidewalk and put it over my head like a veil to protect from the rain but mostly to be anonymous as the town reacted and I chose retreat. Inside the front vestibule of the Inn, I passed the waitresses and Santi who had gathered and ignored their inquiry as to what had happened. The barroom was empty except for a solitary figure in a black turtleneck and jeans on a bar stool at the far end.

"Hello, Caesar," she asked. "Remember me?"

My heart, underneath a cold wet t-shirt, was everywhere at once. Brandy Redfern was my brother Angie's high school girlfriend and my image of nubile, rebellious beauty: a copperhead in cut-off shorts and concert Ts. A girl from a Tom Petty song. A kid of divorce, she'd moved up from Florida and connected with Angie right away. She sat on his lap or rode on his back on their way to the hills to smoke joints and have sex. She was the last person besides me to see Angie alive.

There'd been a fight outside the town pool late in August the summer I was 15. A better-off kid from the other side of town had gotten the best of Angie, and this wasn't supposed to happen, though I wasn't that surprised since Angie had been sullen and distracted of late. After the fight, he took off on his motorbike, but I stuck around to enact some revenge with great emphasis. A little later I found Angie near our hangout beside the train tracks, among the abandoned cars. He and Brandy were arguing with great animation, but I couldn't hear what they were saying. She seemed to be pleading, grabbing at his forearms, which he would yank away. I was about 50 yards away when he slapped her in the face and took off running down the tracks.

I chased him down the tracks and up the gravel embankment around the bend where I caught him on a narrow ridge that snaked alongside a junk yard with a high cyclone fence covered in tarp and topped in barbed wire. I knew what he was doing. He was running away. He'd talked about it for years, of going out to California or somewhere west, where he'd work with his hands and escape all the madness of our town and our home. Angie was our shining prince, and there was immense pressure on him to keep things together. I knew he had cracked that day, and that he was not coming back. I just wanted him to stay or take me with him, and I held him down on that ridge for dear life, until a train whistle blew. I eased off of Angie to wait for the danger to pass - we didn't even walk on that ridge when trains went by - but he wrestled away and kicked me in the face. Stunned by his violence and aware of the danger, I paused in my thoughts of pursuit as Angie scrambled away down the ridge, looking frantically over his shoulder when the train came into view and a guard dog hit the fence, startling Angie and sending him down the gravel slope and into the path of the oncoming train.

I'd be the one to run away soon after that, and the last time I saw Brandy Redfern was when I'd run past her on the train tracks where she had a hand on her cheek. And now she was in my bar asking if I remembered her. I did not speak.

"It's so nice to see you," she said, still with a drop of honey in her accent.

She'd put on a good amount of weight, especially around her hips and chin, and her hair had gone a little dry. But all of her beauty was still there, emanating out of her like it always had, visceral and hypnotic, like the sirens who drove seaworthy ships into the cliffs, though Brandy Redfern was a being of benevolent beauty. Being around her made you fall in rhythm with her breath and crave her attention. All of us had loved her, I believe.

"Hi," I said.

People started pouring into the Inn looking for a place to drink and gather and make sense of the unfolding tragedy.

"Can I be of help?" Brandy asked.

Chapter 17

Brandy grabbed a tray, like she'd worked there for years, and began taking orders. Richie was off that night, and I was alone behind the bar in a room that soon filled to capacity. No one was eating, so the dining area became an extension of the bar. Santi helped behind the bar, and the trio of waitresses plus Brandy worked the floor in both rooms. I was in non-stop motion fixing drinks and pouring pints, but the gist of what happened came to me through the assorted conversations combined with what I already knew.

The freighter carrying natural gas was going too fast and it collided with the 5:15 commuter on the bend in the tracks. There were deaths to be expected, though the only ones being reported early were the conductor and small crew of the freighter as it had been blown to holy hell with no survivors expected. The commuter, not usually crowded at that early hour, had been destroyed up front, where fatalities were expected, and wrecked in back where many injuries were sure to be had. Paramedics were busy helping bodies from the wreckage and notifications of townspeople were being made by phone in case of emergency and in person for the more somber news. I imagined officer Mike being busy that night.

In some ways, it felt like being off site for a sporting event or a battle, where news from the field or the front was delivered to an interested crowd who waited with baited breath. While the event was tragic, the early news was somewhat promising as the early train was not generally crowded and most from our town, at least, preferred the express that ran along the tracks below town, the one closer to the Inn that rattled the window panes upon arrival. Still, names were bandied about in speculation, none that I knew, and it reminded me of anonymity and one of the benefits of being a stranger. Less pain and knowledge of other people's problems. No one I ever heard of would die that day. Or so I thought.

During a lull, Brandy put her elbows up on the bar and leaned forward. "Can you believe this shit?" she asked, her face a riot of empathy and concern, her faint southern accent adding some sweetness to her bitter words.

"Think you might know any of them?" I asked her.

She straightened off the bar. "Me? No," she said, shaking her head. "I've been gone nearly as long as you have."

I wanted to ask her where she'd gone and a hundred other things, too, but the room went silent when Katie Donaghy entered, escorted by an entourage of girlfriends with their arms around her shoulder. They led her to a booth and buffered her within their concern. Even in shock, she was a bright and blond pixie with mystical charms. Not my type, but there was no denying her powers of attraction. Brandy wandered over and asked "What's going on?"

I couldn't make out the reply. She returned a minute later with a stricken look.

"They might need some drinks over there," she said. "Lots."

I poured out five pints of lager and arranged them on a tray. It was then that I realized I hadn't been charging anybody all night. That didn't bother me at all.

"Right back," Brandy said.

The room was warm with body heat and moist air, and at some point Brandy had taken off her thick sweater and was now in a short-sleeved blouse that clung to her shoulders as her body swung back through the room.

"Looks like her husband might be missing," Brandy said with a flick of her head back toward the booth where Katie Donaghy huddled. "Says he takes that train most days and she hasn't heard from him."

I rubbed my chin and thought of Dinny Tuite.

"You know him?" Brandy asked. "Her husband."

"Met him once."

"Nice guy?"

Before I could answer, Mike walked in wearing his dark uniform and cap. His shoulders were soaked, but his hands were clean. His face was flat except for eyes squinted in what looked like agony.

"Remember Brandy Redfern, don't you Mike? Angie's old girlfriend."

She flashed a warm smile, and recognition shook Mike's face. "Oh, yeah," he said. "How's it going?"

Brandy nodded and offered a pleasant smile, appropriate for the moment.

"What's the word?" I asked him.

"Total chaos up there," he said. "Absolute fucking shit show."

"Any news?"

"We got a couple of conductors confirmed, but that's it right now," he said. "Have you seen..."

"She's over there," I said, nodding towards the booth that held Katie Donaghy.

Mike shot me a look of wonder that I ignored, not even sure myself how I knew who he was looking for. He took off his cap and parted the crowd around the booth. Then he led Katie Donaghy out of the bar and into the misty night.

Chapter 18

We stayed open late, though the crowds dwindled as the night wore on. The damage was massive, with wreckage all over the tracks and into the nearby woods, but the topography around the bend didn't lend itself to home building, so the damage was contained to the tracks and the woods. The rain kept the flames from an inferno in the pines. The body count was unclear as the first few cars of the commuter were smithereens of metal and glass. Bone and flesh and blood, too. We'd have to wait for the missing persons to count the dead. I couldn't stop thinking about that little boy waiting on his father.

Brandy stuck around till closing, and we were the last two in the barroom when she blew the wavy bangs from her forehead and settled on a stool.

"Those poor people," she sighed. "God."

"Care for a drink?"

She pursed her lips into a rosebud and nodded three times.

"Whiskey?"

One nod.

I chocked a cocktail glass with ice chips and filled it with two fingers of Wild Turkey. I made myself the same, and we sipped whiskey in silence till our glasses were only ice.

"Hungry?" I asked.

She chuckled a little bit and bounced once on her seat. "You just asked my all-time favorite question."

"Any requests?"

"Really anything would be nice at this point."

"Right back," I said and headed for the kitchen.

"Is there a phone I could use?" she asked to my back.

I pointed to the one hanging on the wall by the waitress station; the one that had been ringing all night but was never answered.

The kitchen was a veritable display of perishables. A restaurant owner's nightmare is a full kitchen at night's end. It's a tough business when your product has a shelf life, but I liked the inherent risk in that, the gamble of sorts. Besides, I'd been on the winning side of things nearly every night since opening.

And I was happy, on this night, not to be sold out of our best offerings at this late hour, under these circumstances.

Santi had refrigerated all the unused menu items, and inside the reach-in was enough food for a family reunion. The hotel pan full of raw lamb chops inspired me to make a dish I used to regularly serve a lovely Reverend and her deacons who had befriended me back in Brooklyn. The Reverend and her deacons had come up from the South as well, like Brandy, and I knew those belles had a taste for all things fried. I also thought some reverence to religion was appropriate on this night.

I cranked up the gas on the deep fryer and seasoned the chops on a clean cutting board. I quartered two lemons. With great efficiency, I set up a station of flour, egg, and bread crumbs in three deep dishes right next to the fryer, which - with wet-hand / dry-hand technique - were visited by each chop and dropped in the fryer where they sizzled for two minutes. I shook the basket and dropped the finished chops on a platter lined with paper towels where they were seasoned with salt and turned onto the ceramic belly of the platter and adorned with a generous squeeze of lemons that sizzled on the crusty, golden surface.

"Well shit," Brandy said when I walked back into the barroom with the stacked platter of fried lamb chops. "You did all that just now?"

"I would've made an anchovy sauce for the side, but that would take too long."

Brandy wrinkled her nose at the idea of anchovy sauce, but I assured her it was good.

"If you say so," she said, leaning over the platter of chops that filled the room with a smell of cooked meat and fried coating.

"Oh, I forgot plates and stuff," I said, making a move for the back.

"Don't even bother," she said, pulling a chop from the platter and biting into it.

I loved that moment of watching someone's reaction to food you've made especially for them.

Her eyes went wide and "Oh my god," she said through a full mouth, which released some heat and garbled words. "So good."

I gave her a clean bar rag to wipe her mouth and pulled a bottle of Chianti Classico from the rack to fill two goblets with ruby red nectar. We sat and ate and drank in the music of moans and laughs and chortles conjured by good food and pleasant company. The wine washed away the mouth feel, tantalizing the taste buds with new, complimentary flavors and clearing the way to begin the experience again. At one point, Brandy smacked me, hard, in the shoulder and let a peel of laughter rip through the room.

When the platter was empty and the wine gone, I fetched a bottle of grappa and poured us two small glasses. I was thinking of how perfect an evening can be with a cocktail, followed by a savory meal with perfect wine, and a digestive at the end. A sense of wellness and serenity settled over me, interrupted by a big breath and the flushed and precious face of Brandy Redfern.

"So," she said as her face reddened and her eyes welled. "We need to talk."

"About what?"

"Well," she said, taking a deep breath and letting it out of her nose. "For starters, you have a nephew. And he's 11 years old."

Chapter 19

Brandy went home shortly after that. But not before telling me that she'd been pregnant back in high school and that the father was Angie. That's what had been bothering him those last weeks, what they'd been fighting about on the tracks that last day when he slapped her and ran off in shame. She wanted an abortion; he wanted them to run away and start a family. After Angie died, Brandy didn't have the heart to abort the baby, so she moved back to Florida to live with her mom near Tallahassee where she became a mother herself and worked waitress jobs at college bars near the state university. She named the boy Charles, but he went by Charlie. She'd named him after her own father, but, according to Brandy, he looked like a Stiles.

Another fucking Stiles. I sat in the barroom after Brandy went home, sipping grappa and breaking my no-smoking rule, swarmed with warmth and dread and possibilities. What I felt most of all, though, was a sense of responsibility. Charlie had been getting in trouble at school back in Florida, so Brandy moved him up here for a fresh start, for both of them, and to live with her father, but he had a stroke over the summer and had to be put into an assisted living center and sell his house to cover the costs, which were still piling up. Brandy and Charlie took an apartment near the Meadowlands. She attended classes at a community college and worked in a diner; he hated everything about New Jersey. I couldn't help but think that the poor boy was a victim of the Stiles' family curse without even knowing he was one of us.

My mother believed our family was cursed because her mother came to America in the usual way but not for the usual purposes, to immigrate and start a new life. My mother's mother came from Sicily to America to kill a man. Which she did. And because of that, my mother believed that our family had been identified by the bad spirits. When she first told me all this, in her dying days, I thought it was the ramblings of a delusional woman doped up on the black market morphine I'd been feeding her prodigious quantities of, but our family sure had its share of bad things by that point, as Angie was dead and Sallie incarcerated and our father run off and never heard from anymore. And then there was the fact that, before my mother's illness brought me home, I'd been living with a young woman outside of Lafayette, Louisiana - A Creole child named Carmen, granddaughter of a Sicilian mysteriously murdered in New Orleans who fit the exact description of the man my mother explained her mother had come here to search America for and kill. Which she did. Shit that fantastic makes you believe in the bad spirits.

It was also my mother's belief that the curse could be broken simply by resisting the urge to run, which I'd been doing half of my life. But now I was home, ambivalent about her wishes and this idea of home. I was giving it a shot, and now I had another one from our line to consider, a kid named Charlie Redfern who I had yet to meet but inspired a grand idea to spare him his fate as I passed out in the studio above the barroom that had become my home away from home.

Chapter 20

News the next day was somber but threaded with relief as the town itself got off relatively easy in the accident. Of the 20 confirmed missing, only two were believed to be ours, both non-natives: one a divorced and childless actuary living in an apartment complex on the edge of town; the other was Dinny Tuite.

Mike came into the bar around 6:00, out of uniform and in the company of a fit, mid-50s guy with short, white hair, pink lips, a papery face and a nylon jacket. It took Mike about ten minutes to make it through the decent crowd as each group wanted a word with the local hero who had the latest on the tragic events. The guy with him snapped gum and didn't bother with any of the other patrons, keeping his eyes on me the whole time, as if we had some business to discuss. Richie was off for the second straight night, and the crowd was pretty good on both sides of the house.

Mike, finally free, motioned with his head down to the far end of the bar by the waitress station where nobody stood. After fixing a couple of orders, I met him and his companion.

"This is Dick Donaghy," Mike said to me. "Katie's father."

"Sorry about your son-in-law," I said.

Dick Donaghy let out something akin to a chuckle and looked around the bar. "I'm not going to lie to you," he said, his small and stark blue eyes now on me. "I never liked that fucking guy she married."

"All right," I said.

I didn't like grown men who chewed gum.

I remembered the Dick Donaghy type - hard asses who coached teams like drill sergeants or yelled like maniacs from the sidelines, suburban feudal lords looking for a fight on a sunny afternoon. I wondered why Mike had brought this man to me.

"The thing is Caes," Mike said, "Mr. Donaghy here believes that his son-in-law isn't so much dead as he is missing."

"And how's that?"

Dick Donaghy took a walk and feigned interest as he inspected the barroom and Mike leaned toward me in confidence.

"There's no sign of his body, as of yet, at the scene, though it's possible, like a few others of the missing, that there will be no signs, if you know what I mean."

I guessed that some were just evaporated in the blast. "OK," I said.

"But Katie claims that there's something up with their finances. A lot of missing funds that can't be accounted for."

"How much?"

Mike leaned closer. "We're talking millions, Caes."

"She found all this out today?"

Mike had a whimsical look on his face when he explained that Katie and Dinny had been having marital problems, which jibed with what Richie had told me about Dinny Tuite not being popular in town with anyone. He said that Katie had been expecting him to leave at some point, so she'd been keeping an eye on the money. And now much of it was gone.

"Lovely," I said.

"What a prince," Mike said. "Huh?"

I said nothing as Dick Donaghy returned from his stroll to join Mike tucked up against my bar. I went off to fill a few orders and returned.

"The thing is, Caes, if this guy's making a run, he's gonna do it now, or at least soon, so he has to be caught soon."

"Caught?"

"Yes," Mike confirmed. "Caught."

"And I want you to catch the bastard," Dick Donaghy blurted and pointed a little finger at me. "And bring him to me."

His face had gone a little ruddy; his lips flat and fishy. White spittle gathered at the side of his mouth. I wasn't interested in anything to do

with the man or his daughter or the man to whom she was married. At
that point I wasn't even interested in the man his daughter was clearly
fucking, my oldest friend in the world.

"That's not what I do," I said to Dick Donaghy and then turned my
eyes on Mike.

Dick Donaghy curled up his face and walked out the door. Mike wore
a mask of incredulity. "Come on, Caes," he said. "Hear us out on this."

"You're the damn policeman," I said to him.

"And I'll be working seven days a week for the next month, until we
get this whole mess cleared up and resolved, get all these investigators
out of town. I got no time for it."

"And I do?"

"Look, Caes, you've got a knack for this shit. I told you that. All you
gotta do is look around a bit, see if you can find a trail or anything. If so,
I'll find some time to jump in with you - we'd be like partners, you know,
Starsky & Hutch."

Mike smiled, referencing our favorite detective show from when we
were kids. It felt like we were still kids. And we weren't alone in that.
Lots of grown men acted like children.

Mike pulled out a check from his back pocket and put it on the bar.
"It's from Mr. Donaghy, a starter's fee just for looking around."

It was a signed check for $10,000.

"And you actually find the guy," Mike said, "Dicky there will give you
ten times that amount."

I thought of Brandy Redfern and my nephew.

"And how would I start this looking around?"

"I've got you covered, Caes," Mike said, a boyish smile bouncing
around his face and eyes. "You remember my brother Rob, right?"

I nodded.

"He works out of his home office in Fairview these days. Go see him
tomorrow morning. I'll let him know you're coming. He knows people at
the firm where Tuite worked. Put you in touch with some people."

I tapped the check on the bar.

Chapter 21

Mike's brother lived a few town's over. It was a swanky hamlet with a lot of brick homes and colonials. Flat, winding roads with no sidewalks. Green, green lawns that came right up to the street. A cop cruiser pulled up alongside me about a quarter mile into town, in the dappled sunlight of quivering maple leaves. When I told the inquiring officer where I was going, he gave me a ride to the sprawling white colonial with Chez McBride on the mailbox. I walked the long driveway lined with sporting equipment and things to ride. A backboard and hoop hung above the three-car garage. Over a wooden fence was a large yard with a trampoline, swimming pool, and a batting cage.

A stone path led to the front door with a lion's head knocker. I grabbed the ring in the lion's mouth when the door opened to a raven-haired beauty in workout clothes and a baby on her hip. I was in all denim with the collar up on the jacket.

"Hi," she said, sort of breathless. "You must be Mike's friend."

"I am," I said.

"I'm Michele," she said extending her free hand. "Rob's wife."

I shook Michele's soft hand and smiled at her handsome baby.

"And this is Connor," she said.

"Hello, Connor," I said. "And how are you?"

He tucked his face into the nape of his mother's neck. I envied him.

"Come in," Michele said and stepped out of the doorway.

The foyer was open and full of light and hung with a large chandelier. A dozen pairs of shoes and sneakers in various sizes were scattered in the vestibule. Rooms branched out in many directions. Kitchen noise came through the open doorway straight back where I imagined a domestic cleaning up the breakfasts that filled the kids who wore the sneakers and put all that sporting equipment to use.

"Want me to take off my shoes?" I asked.

"Um," she said, looking at my mountain boots. "No. That's OK."

She gave me directions and said her goodbyes as she pointed through the wide entrance to an immaculate, carefully-curated living room of sofas and curtains and glass tables that appeared to never be used. A door on the far end of the living room, across a plush carpet, led to a high-ceilinged recreation area with a full-size billiard's table and a smaller bumper pool unit in the back. A dart board was on the wall, and a video game meant for an arcade was tucked between the windows that faced the yard. A full oak bar, with taps up front and a stocked, premium shelf behind, ran along the far wall. Leather Lazy-boy chairs spotted the room, and a felt-topped card table was surrounded by four folding chairs. A scent of cigar smoke and air freshener lingered in the silence.

Yet another door had to be passed before finding Mike's brother who sat behind a desk in a spacious Florida room with windows on all three sides and sliding glass doors that opened to a slate patio in the backyard. He was at his large desk, partitioned by a battalion of monitors, studying the screens with a hand gently over his mouth. I cleared my throat.

Rob McBride stood up and broke into the healthiest of smiles. I didn't know many happy people, which made them easy to identify.

"What's going on, Caesar Stiles?" he said, waving me toward his control center. Rob was sleight by Mike's standards but trim and of polished skin and teeth. His soft brown hair looked trimmed on a regular basis and was the exact same length he wore as the fine and extraordinarily confident young man he once was and, it appeared, remained. He wore the collar up on a lavender golf shirt with a polo player for an emblem. He hadn't changed really at all, and I told him so as we shook hands over a monitor.

He said the same about me and offered me a seat in the leather chair off to the side of his desk. There were lots of pictures of family and friends, golf memorabilia and knick-knacks, a set of clubs and a fake putting green in the back. He'd apparently attended Georgetown

University, and lots of framed acknowledgments for civic duty hung on the wall.

"What'cha watching?" I asked him. "Brady Bunch?"

"Stock market," he said. "You follow the Street?"

"And what street is that?"

"Wall Street."

"No," I smiled, "but I've heard you've done pretty well there."

Mike had bragged that his brother was worth an ungodly amount of money, but Rob McBride shrugged and looked a bit uncomfortable about his little brother's big mouth. "Mike told me about all that you'd been up to," he said. "That's incredible."

Now it was my turn to shrug.

"Said you're going to write a book about it," he added.

It occurred to me that a secret of success, for some truly talented people, besides work ethic and smarts, is the ability to make lesser people feel like equals in your presence. I found his modesty impressive.

"I don't know about that."

"And you're doing some detective work?"

I laughed at the absurdity. "Now that I really don't know about. I'm just doing a favor for Mike because, you know, he asked me to."

"You know something," Rob said, his eyes now earnest. "He wasn't the same after you left. You were such good friends that it was like a part of him ran away with you. He had girlfriends, lots of them, but never really any good guy friends like you."

I never thought of that. I was too busy trying to survive, worrying about my mother, wondering about my father, suffering over Angie, to think about the one real friend I'd left behind.

"Yeah," I said. "It's good to see him again."

Rob made a steeple out of his fingers and smiled. "Remind me. Why are you two looking for this guy?"

"I dunno," I said. "Has to do with the train accident, and Katie Donaghy, and her father, I guess."

"Dick Donaghy," Rob said, shaking his head. "What a dick."

"Not at all," I said.

Rob smiled. "I don't know the guy you're after, but he worked on a team within a very successful firm."

"A team?"

"Yeah, a lot of big firms break down into specialized units to focus on certain sectors, like oil or agriculture or pharma. Following?"

I could really give a shit but nodded anyway.

"This guy Tuite," Rob said, his eyes darting toward the screen, "worked with a small group run by a guy named Ira Zeiler."

Rob cracked up a bit at the thought.

"And what's so funny about that?"

"This guy Ira is sort of infamous in financial circles."

"And why's that?"

"Well, he's a bit of an oddball. A free spirit, I guess."

"Is he good at what he does?"

"One of the best," Rob said, with a respectful nod. "Year in year out, guy makes money. Big time."

"And Dinny Tuite worked for him?"

"That's what I heard. Recruited by Ira right out of college."

"He'll talk to me?"

"If he knows I sent you."

Chapter 22

Rob McBride placed a call on my behalf, and his raven-haired and lovely wife saved the local police the effort of driving me out of town. She dropped me at the train station, and I caught a Manhattan-bound express that rattled over rails in a familiar manner, the click and clack filling the empty car as the tree line whipped past and blurred my watery reflection in the window. I missed my shining brother all the time, like a severed limb, and trains made the loss particularly acute. It's why I dumped the train motif in the old Inn, but trains in commuter towns were hard to avoid. The irony was that I liked them, too; the romance and mystery of moving at great speeds across great swaths of land simply as a passenger. I liked the sounds, too; the whistles and warning bells and steady clatter like a metronome keeping time.

I dozed off and dreamed of my father telling me the story of John Henry, the steel driving man, who challenged a machine to a contest of laying down track, and how John Henry had won by a single spike then died on the spot. I asked my father if it was a happy ending or a sad ending. "He won, now, didn't he?" my father said, tussling my hair into a nest. I could never make up my mind about the ending.

The train whistle blew as we entered the caverns below Penn Station. The corridors were uncrowded at midday, and I caught a downtown subway to Wall Street. Lower Manhattan was narrow and charming and reminiscent of old New York, except for the Twin Towers that loomed like giant markers of modern America. Their size and symbolism made me uncomfortable, hardly able to look up at the dizzying masses of metal and glass that blocked the sky. The audacity of the idea matched the physical intimidation of the buildings.

I entered Tower #1 and its immense, light-filled lobby of marble and murals and potted fichus trees. I found the elevator banks that led to the 52nd Floor, where I walked around silent hallways looking for a name of the firm and the suite number I'd been given by Mike's brother. Eventually, I settled on the wooden door marked by a reversed New York Knicks jersey with the name Mason arched over a large 14. The sound of music eked out from behind the solid door; I knocked but no one answered, so I let myself in.

The empty and light-filled room resembled the aftermath of a party: full waste bins, real plates and glasses and silverware scattered on desks and cabinets, the smell of smoke, discarded coffee cups and cans of soda, fizzled energy worming around the edges of the room. The walls were decorated with sports memorabilia and gold records and posters of white women in bathing suits and black men in motion as athletes or musicians. It looked like a fraternity penthouse.

The offices had wooden doors and glass walls and big windows in back with dramatic views of the Hudson River and the shoreline of New Jersey. A conference room had a picked-over buffet with plenty of leftovers in hot trays and on cold platters. I followed the music to a closed door in the center of all the erstwhile action where a man about my age in a dress shirt and tie leaned back in a leather chair, bobbed his head hard to the music as he lit a massive joint.

He coughed when I knocked on the glass, spouting a plume of sweet-smelling ganja into the room and under the door. He wiped away the smoke and waved me in. There was an open bottle of Absolute vodka on the messy desk. The music was loud and had a bombastic yet cohesive arrangement with the most audacious lyrics I'd ever heard in all of my life: ones that argued about not wanting to be called "nigga" while using the word repeatedly throughout.

I couldn't believe what I was hearing. It was brilliant and shocking, confrontational and brave. A forbidden word turned on its head. Rebel music writ large. I assumed the song was meant to match the ethos of the unusual man sitting there disheveled and decadent in the middle of the day in the heart of America's largest financial sector. I also assumed he was the man I came to see.

Ira Zeiler turned off the music, backhanded his mouth, and offered me the joint. His suit jacket was off and his shirt wrinkled and loosened at the collar, like it was 1:00 in the morning, not the afternoon. His expression was a mix of weary and elated. His eyes were flat and glassy as a placid sea.

"You like that song or what?" he asked with provocation, the joint held out in my direction.

I refused the joint but nodded at the question. "Might be the best rock and roll song of all time."

He sucked his teeth and said, "Shit. That ain't rock, it's rap, brother. You don't even know the difference?"

The little rap I'd heard was some guy rhyming over a programmed beat or one made by a mouth spitting into a hand. Clearly, I was not familiar with the genre's evolution.

"Got a lot of sound going," I said, "like a full rock band. And those lyrics are about as transgressive as it gets. That's rock and roll, at least the best of it, orchestrated noise and a fuck you message."

Ira Zeiler's face admitted my point and then grew curious. He stood to look me over, boots and denim and hair.

"How you know a serious player like Rob Mac B.?" he asked.

"Grew up together."

"No shit?"

I didn't answer rhetorical questions.

He sat back down and motioned toward a cushioned chair that fronted his desk. In the corner was a life-sized cut-out of a muscular and big-eyed black man in a Knicks uniform wearing the same #14 jersey that hung on the front door of the suites. The rest of the room, except for the framed degrees from Harvard and the University of Pennsylvania, had a similar high school jock vibe with a thread of menace in a lot of headless Michael Jordan images (one of the missing heads was pasted near the crotch of #14).

He saw me looking at a half-eaten pastrami sandwich on his desk and asked if I was hungry. I was. We walked out of the THC fumes of his office into the fresher air and light of the conference room. Ira Zeiler, bottle of Absolute in hand, hit the beverage station for a glass of ice then grabbed a seat at the far head of the conference table. I helped myself to a pile of roast beef on rye with a healthy dollop of horseradish sauce and a bag of salty chips. There were higher-end offerings available, but they'd been under the heat lamp too long. I took a bottle of seltzer water and my sandwich down to where Ira Zeiler sat, a silhouette in the halo of blue sky of a clear October afternoon. He poured himself generous vodka on the rocks.

"Where is everybody?" I asked.

"Split," he said. "Our desk trades overseas, mostly in Asia, so we done by, shit, noon New York."

"And why are you still here?"

"I'm the boss. I stick around to watch the other markets, get a jump on tomorrow. Keep the shit correct."

I kept silent, hoping he'd keep talking.

"Besides," he said, squeezing his glass. "I'm working through some shit right now. Know what I'm saying?"

He poured some vodka from the bottle on to the carpeted floor.

The street rhythm to his speech patterns threw me. They reminded me of Dinny Tuite's way of speaking, but not as smooth or natural. More forced. I ate some roast beef sandwich and thought about this oddity in front of me.

"Where'd you grow up?" I asked.

"Great Neck, out in Nassau, Strong Island. You know, Greenwich for Jews."

I got very little of that statement. Sometimes I felt so out of context it was like I'd been on Mars for the past 12 years.

"So Dinny Tuite worked for you?"

Ira Zeiler rattled his head and straightened his spine, as if I'd just hit him with a bolt of lightning. "You know, Dinny? The fuck? I thought Rob McBride sent you?"

"He did."

"The fuck that got to do with Dinny Tuite?"

I looked at Ira Zeiler's glass of cold vodka. "You two were close, yeah?"

"Hell, yeah," he said, emotion swelling in the center of his face. "He was my fucking boy. I loved that motherfucker."

He rambled on from there about how he'd spotted Dinny's talent and style at a college fair, recruited him out of Fordham and mentored him on Wall Street in his renegade outfit of outsiders who won no popularity contests but made money hand over fist every quarter. He explained how they did it, but I don't give a shit about how people make money, honest or dishonest, though I did take stock in the fact that Dinny was exceptional at his job: "A straight up rainmaker" in the puzzling vernacular of Ira Zeiler.

"You haven't heard from him?" I asked.

"What? Since when? What?"

"Since the train accident."

"Fuck you talking about?" Ira Zeiler asked and looked around an empty room to imply he may be in the presence of a crazy man.

"There's a theory that he may not be dead but only missing."

For the first time, Ira Zeiler looked at me like I was the one who spoke funny. "I'm sorry, man. Who in the fuck are you again?"

"I've been asked by the family of Dinny's wife to look into his possible disappearance as opposed to his death."

Ira Zeiler sat up straight and scrunched his face as if something smelled terribly. "Those fucking people right there can go fuck on themselves."

He tapped the table, hard, with the hand not choking the Absolute bottle.

"You know the Donaghys then?"

"Shhh...I went to the wedding. Was in D's party. It was clear then that they thought she was too good for him, even then, all them sisters and her snotty ass friends looking down their noses, and that mother fucking father. Fucking prick, man. Boring ass wedding, too. Bunch of drunk white people. Bagpipes and shit. Some fucked up Irish ass dancing. Lamest fucking party I ever hit."

"You know of any problems Dinny was having with his wife?"

"He didn't talk about that shit, no, but I knew he wasn't happy. I knew that."

"And how'd you know that?"

"We a bunch of mutants around here. You know? Dudes who start in the wee wee hours of the morning and done for the day when most people heading out to lunch. That leaves an afternoon for all sorts of mischief, you know, when the rest of the world at their desks or whatnot. Dinny always the first one out the door, but he never went wildin' with us."

"With you where?"

"Come on, man," he said. "Young men in this fucking town with time and plenty of money in our pockets? Where you think we go?"

"Museums?"

Ira Zeiler laughed and then grew contemplative. "But Dinny never joined."

"Maybe that wasn't his style."

"Shit," Ira Zeiler laughed. "Nah, Dinny was a player. He loved the pussy and the pussy loved him. He had that thing about him, you know? Magnetism or some shit. Used to drive me crazy. We spent a week in Hong Kong together, and let me tell you that dude almost didn't come back. It's just that he kept his shit on the down low. I turn around, and he be gone, just ghosting, man."

"Maybe he had a girlfriend or something?"

Ira Zeiler looked at me, his eyes squinted in drunken suspicion. "The fuck would I help you for? You out to fuck with my boy and shit. You on their side, not his."

"I'm not on anyone's side," I said. "Though the only one of the Donaghy's I've met is the father, and I hear you on that. Complete fucking prick. I'm just trying to find out if Dinny's alive or not."

"Alive? Really? Dinny? Come on. How is that even possible?" Now Ira Zeiler was less cartoonish and full of a hope that could be of help.

"At this point, it seems probable," I said. "There's no body and a reason to get gone, if you know what I mean."

"I do. I do. Wait here."

Ira Zeiler left his vodka bottle on the table and swaggered out of the conference room. I ate my sandwich and watched tug boats churn through the waters off lower Manhattan and airplanes pierce the blue sky not so far overhead.

I finished the sandwich and seltzer and chips, and was taking a cup of coffee when Ira Zeiler returned. "Here," he said, a little harried and uplifted. "This might help."

He sat back down and slid a Polaroid picture of a topless Latina, fists on her hips and her heavy breasts lunging forward like guard dogs. A defiant half smile split her wide mouth. She looked bad. And good. And appeared to be in the backroom of a nightclub or maybe a strip joint. Lots of mirrors and lights. Her hair all layered. Makeup on her face. Glittery ribbons extending from her closed hands.

"This his girlfriend?" I asked.

"I dunno, but it was in his desk, bottom drawer, under a bunch of files and shit."

"You went through his things?"

He put both hands on the table. "Part of what I do after everyone goes home," he said.

I didn't say anything.

"I have to make sure my crew is on the up and up and shit. I don't like to, G, but I gots to. Got a lot of young cats in here with plenty of money in they pockets. You know? Like I said, we mutants, lot of enemies. One fuck up, and we out. SEC on us like white on rice. Know what I'm sayin?"

"Dinny clean?"

"As a mother fucking whistle," he said and snapped. "Neatest office in the house. No drugs. No nothing. Just that."

"Let me ask you something."

"Aight."

"Had Dinny been acting different as of late, you know, distracted or distant?"

"Yeah, man, he had," Ira said, as if coming to a conclusion. "I thought maybe he was going to make a move. Thas' why I went through his desk, too, just to make sure he wasn't sitting on any offers or no shit like that. See if he was packing up his shit and getting out of dodge."

"Was he?"

"Hard to tell. Cat so organized."

"He ever talk about being unhappy at home?"

"No, but I knew he hated that town, said that on more than one occasion. But nothing about his old lady, but there ain't no picture of her anywhere on that desk. And there was this one time, last spring, after we took some clients out and Dinny got drunk as shit, I mean fucking shit-faced wasted, and I was stuffing him in a car to get his ass home, he was mumbling some shit about his wife fucking a cop in town. Some dude she dated back in high school."

I hardly reacted though my head started spinning.

"Can I take it?" I asked, picking up the Polaroid.

Ira Zeiler fell into a chair near his bottle of vodka. He put his hands behind and his head and kicked back. "Only if you promise to put me in touch with that motherfucker when you find his ass."

I promised that I would.

Chapter 23

I walked out of the heights of the World Trade Center and went underground. A PATH train whisked me under the Hudson River and into Jersey City, from where I caught a livery cab to Bayonne and Cha Cha Porter's place. Trying to be a detective without much local knowledge was hard, so I had to rely on people in the know. If this lovely Latina was dancing in Jersey, like I suspected she was, he might be the man in the know.

Glory Social was crowded and open to the public this Friday afternoon. The room was full of Teamsters and cigarette smoke and the joyous banter of a fledgling weekend after a long week of physical labor. Fat Elvis shot pool in back with a crew of stevedores. The monster loomed behind the bar, popping caps on long necks for the crowd that ran four deep.

Not a female in the joint, but the room had a good vibe, men of various ages and races, who bonded because they worked with their hands and shared the same union benefits. A jukebox kicked out a bumpy Chuck Berry tune, an evergreen number that softened the edges of a room full of hard men. I caught the bartender's eye, and he chucked his huge head toward the back of the room. I waved; he nodded. I cut through the crowded room and said "nice shot" to Fat Elvis after he banked an eight ball into a side pocket backed by a pile of money.

Cha Cha Porter was on a sparse patio of cracked cement in a gathering of men around a picnic table who were a little older, a little better dressed and less taxed by physical labor than the men inside. Cha Cha was dressed particularly nice, in a black cardigan over a beige silk T, black slacks and a black cap low above his eyes. The diamond in his left ear twinkled in the autumn sun like the shards of light fining on the inlet that split the shipping terminal and its industrial skyline. The brackish air was cut with the smell of natural gas. Cargo ships skulked through the churning waters. Thin clouds zig-zagged the sky.

A short, older guy with a gin blossom nose and Brylcreemed hair was telling a garbled story out of the side of his mouth. Everyone looked amused and aware of the outcome, probably a tale told a thousand times about a familiar figure. One of those stories that never gets old, if you're in on the context. I wasn't, so I waited for the finish, the obligatory laughter, the nostalgic slaps on the back and then the din as the laughter fades. Cha Cha Porter excused himself from the table as if he knew I was there all along. He approached smiling, his chin up, and shook my hand.

"Thought I might see you again," he said.

"And why's that?"

"Don't know. Just a hunch. You believe in those, don't ya? Hunches."

"I do."

"Thought so," he smiled and motioned with his head to a small Astroturf platform toward the water where a trio of shiny golf clubs leaned into a metal stand next to a bucket of dimpled white balls. "You play?" he asked, grabbing a club.

I shook my head and sat in the lone plastic chair next to the platform. With his back to me, Cha Cha flipped some balls out of the bucket, arranged his stance, took a slow back swing and sculled a ball into the water where it skipped across the surface and sank.

"Damn hardest game in the world," he admitted while fixing another ball for practice. This one sailed high and far, and Cha Cha lifted his cap to watch it with great admiration, holding his twisted torso finish, as the little white ball peaked and then descended into the water with a splash. "There you go," he said to himself. "Best damn game in the world, too."

He hit a couple more balls with mixed results.

"You have some information for me," he asked, his back still turned and his practice in progress.

"Not yet," I said, "but I think I'm on to something."

"Well, that's good," Cha Cha said and sliced a ball far to the right that missed the water altogether. It bounced down a concrete tarmac and disappeared under some discarded storage units. "So then what brings you here this fine afternoon?"

"I thought maybe you could help me with something."

His back shuddered in laughter but no sound came. He picked a ball clean off the turf and sent it sailing for the sun. Before it came down, he turned around and addressed me face to face, his cap pushed back high on his straight and short hairline.

"What would that be?"

I pulled out the picture of the topless Latina and handed it to him. "Well, hello, Mommy," he said with a pleased smile. "Who is this?"

"I don't know, but I'm looking for someone I believe to be her boyfriend."

"Lucky him," Cha Cha said. "And what makes you think I could be of help with that?"

"I dunno," I said. "A hunch."

Cha Cha showed a lot of teeth in his smile. He coupled his palms over the club in front of him and perched on it like a cane, his head raised in expectation. He was tall as me but thicker all around. His eyes hard but not cruel. I knew to be careful.

"She dances somewhere accessible from the city, and I'm thinking you might have some ideas as to where."

"And how would I know that?"

"I know what you do."

"And what exactly is that?"

"Let's call it vice, to be polite."

"Your friend the cop tell you that?"

"He did."

"Why didn't you tell me a police officer brought you here last time?"

"You didn't ask," I said. "Besides, he only brought me as a friend."

"You friends with coppers?"

"Just one."

"And is this copper friend of yours outside again waiting for you."

"You'd know if he was."

Cha Cha Porter laughed. "And you know that I'm not a man to be fucked with?"

"I also know that you're smarter than they are."

"Let me ask you something," he said, a gleam entering his eye. "You got any issue with my affairs?"

"Not necessarily."

"Why not?"

"Vice is part of life."

"True, but I meant the 'not necessarily' part."

"Depends on how you go about your business."

Cha Cha Porter took a big step forward and poked me in the chest. "Exactly. That's exactly correct. Smart man right here," he said, turning his head to address an imaginary crowd. "I knew it all along."

A breeze picked up. A seagull screeched and went with the wind. A cloud covered the sun and things got cool. A door opened and the cacophony from inside interrupted our alfresco solitude. The same craggy voice from before that told the story informed Cha Cha that they had a tee-time in 20 minutes.

"How you know this girl in Jersey and not the city?" Cha Cha asked me holding the picture up for me to study. "Lot more talent in the city."

I poked one of her hands. "Tassels," I said. "Don't need them in New York, but you do in Jersey."

"My man," Cha Cha said with a fraternal smile. "You really think you going to be able to help me with my little problem?"

I nodded.

"I'm gonna do you a solid then," Cha Cha said. "Wait out front. Bones be there in a minute."

Chapter 24

It must have been near closing time at Glory Social as the parking lot exodus filled the air with fumes from large engines of American pickup trucks. I imagine their policy at the club was adjusted to semi-private, Teamsters only, on Friday afternoons. A place for the working men to unwind among their own for a while after a long week. The men were all festive and lit, on their way home or on to a night of drinking at other locations. Most seemed to be after the latter, piling into trucks with Styrofoam roadies spilling suds over the sides.

I was finishing my third smoke under the canopy of flags when the monster bartender/messenger ambled up in a navy pea coat with an unlit Pall Mall between his teeth. His hand weighed as much as an encyclopedia. We didn't exchange names, though I inferred he went by Bones. I followed Bones to his car, a comfortable Lincoln with plush leather seats and a nice sound system that kicked in with a turn of the ignition.

The Blues Hour played on a jazz station out of Newark, a jaunty Freddie King instrumental that my buddy Macie Turner used to cover back in Texas and the circuit we traveled together around the lower southwest through Mississippi and Louisiana and Texas. Bones lowered his window and lit the cigarette, bobbed his big head just one time.

"Which of the Kings do you like?" I asked him apropos of nothing, if you weren't into the blues.

"Albert," he said, his voice not as bottomed-out as I remembered.

He looked at me.

"Freddy," I said, a finger at the radio.

Bones nodded and put the car in gear. Neither of us had to acknowledge that we didn't care for B.B. as much. Too flashy and friendly for our kind.

The long, cool Lincoln rolled out of the parking lot toward the expressway.

"And what's our story?" I asked.

"Mr. Porter asked me to give you a ride."

I didn't ask where we were going, but it was clear fairly soon that we weren't going directly home after he put a neatly bound stack of single dollar bills on the arm rest between us. Along an access road parallel to the state turnpike, in the swampy shadows of the Meadowlands, we pulled into the parking lot of a brick building with the black and white silhouette of a woman's figure, curvy legs raised in the air, illuminated on a white sign that read Baby Dolls.

Bones pulled into a parking spot in the back of the lot, lit another cigarette and looked at the stack of bills. "Buy you a drink?" I asked.

He blew smoke out the window. I crossed through what felt like a used car lot and nodded at an overweight and uninspired bouncer crushing a wooden stool. Van Halen's "Ice Cream Man" crackled out of speakers that were ready to blow, and the dingy room was a frenzy of flying dollars and inebriated working men lunging over each other toward the center stage where a peroxide-blond blasted a can of whipped cream between her legs. I circled the room and approached an abandoned bar in the far corner where I handed the young, pompadoured tender a $20 from my own wallet and showed him the picture of Dinny Tuite's girlfriend. He shook his head without hesitation and pocketed my money.

I had a hard time imagining Dinny Tuite, in his tailored suits and street smarts, among this crowd of DPW workers, landscapers, and construction crews busy blowing half-a-week's pay on a slutty burlesque show.

I returned to the car and suggested a more upscale location to Bones, and he took me to three strip joints over the next 90 minutes. I called

Richie from a payphone and asked him to run the show until I arrived and to tell Santi to go with the straight menu, no specials tonight. He said Officer McBride had already been in looking for me. I wasn't surprised.

The last joint we hit was in a quiet quarter of Mattison, of old Victorian homes and brick row houses where the wealthy once lived when the city was a manufacturing hub in the previous century. It was run down now, but not as decrepit as other parts of the city, the well-built structures able to withstand the creeping decay of financial desolation. A detached small Victorian with a peeling facade and wraparound porch had an empty lot on each side and parking in back. The windows were darkened by internal curtains with the white glow of a martini glass shape in one frame and the script neon name of a Dominican beer in the other. Bones pulled up curbside and nodded.

"This might be the place," he said.

I was addled somewhat by a number of beers and exposure to a lot of flesh over a short period of time. I also had a lot of singles to spend, so I crossed the mottled yard and went up the steps and through the front door into a barroom that felt like a grand hotel. The long living room, by original design, was dimly lit with a wooden bar down one end and small, round tables throughout the spacious floor plan faintly illuminated by gleaming chandeliers. Two of the tables had men in suits being entertained by young and brown women in panties, their nipples topped by sparkling tassels.

"Table service only," the bartender told me. He was a hard Latino with a waxed mustache and slicked back hair in a burgundy, silk dress shirt with sleeves rolled up on his tight forearms.

"You know this girl?" I asked, holding out the Polaroid.

He flashed his eyes absently over the photo.

"Table service only," he said again, noticeably less friendly than his original less-than-friendly self.

I sat at a table far away from the other men, by dark curtains in a lonely corner. Through a beaded doorway, a petite Latina sauntered in my direction with a smile that said she'd been expecting me. She extended a small hand and sat on my lap.

"My name is Flower," she whispered in my ear, "but my lovers call me Flor."

Flor's hair was the color of wet sand and she smelled like chocolate. Her round ass felt great on my lap and her perky tits worked just fine. She twisted a braid of my hair and asked if I wanted some champagne. I nodded and before my erection completed, the bartender delivered a bucket of ice plunged with a popped bottle of Vueve Cliquot, two glasses in his hand.

"Das one hundred dollars," he said as Flor, below the table, made slow circles with a finger on the tip of my cock. Sounded like a deal to me. I handed him the rest of Cha Cha's singles and some of my own money. He put the glasses on the table and disappeared through the beaded doorway.

"You want some coke?" she whispered in my ear.

I shook my head.

"X?"

I shook my head and nodded at the champagne bottle.

Flor poured our drinks and teased me in a way that left me spellbound. When the champagne was finished and she suggested, in a breathy whisper, that we go upstairs, I stood up so fast she nearly fell to the floor.

She led me by her tiny hand and her tick-tock ass to the front foyer and up a stairwell lit by Christmas lights. And it felt like Christmas morning to a man who had been denied such wondrous moments as a kid. There was the faint chatter of couples from the bedrooms we passed on the way down a long hallway. In front of a doorway at the end, Flor whispered, "Wait here," and went inside.

I stood in the threshold, bristling with anticipation, waiting for the door to open. For something to do, I unlaced my boots for quick removal and just finished the second shoe when the door opened slowly to no one and dim light.

"Come, baby," Flor said from behind the door.

ANDREW COTTO

I was already breathing hard as I entered, my loosened boots jarred by thick carpet. Flor slipped from behind the door, hit the light and closed the door on her way out. My erection died in the face of two hard Latinos in matching gray Dickie's shirts and pants, prison muscles and prison tattoos on their forearms and necks and faces; one had an industrial tool box; the other a sawed-off shotgun. A twin bed was covered in a durable tarp.

Chapter 25

I officially quit girls from the sex trade and stared down the nubbed-barrel of the shotgun. The smell of ozone indicated it had been fired recently. The barrel motioned toward the far wall, away from the door, and I obliged. The barrel told me to turn around and face the wall; I did. A hand flashed in my back pocket to remove my bill fold and the Polaroid. I thought of the knife, loose in my boot, not that it would do me any good against a shotgun. Nobody spoke. Sweat spread across my back, and my head raced for a plan of escape. The windows were barred. Someone answered a knock on the door.

"Turn around," the bartender said as he walked in with intense eyes and flared nostrils, his jaw rippling and snapping on a piece of gum. He locked the door and spoke quick words in Spanish to the two men; they relaxed their instruments and stood behind the bartender with hands crossed at their crotches, chins up and squinted eyes on me.

The bartender held up my billfold in one hand and the picture in the other.

"You don't have ID, Esse?"

I shook my head.

"The fuck are you then?"

"Anthony Mason," I said.

The bartender huffed some air from his nose. "Like the dude from the Knicks?"

I nodded.

"Where'd you get this?" he asked, shaking the Polaroid.

"Belongs to a guy I know."

"What guy?"

"Guy I know."

"Oh. OK, then," the bartender said, a contemplative frown tipping his head back and forth. "What you doing with it?"

"I heard she was a great fuck," I said. "Came to find out for myself."

The bartender and I studied each other.

"That's funny," he said. "Cause she don't work here. Never has. Works somewhere else we got though."

"Oh," I said. "My mistake then."

"I'll say," he said with the contemplative frown now paired with a nod.

He spoke in Spanish again, and the two men approached me without hesitation.

"You move," the bartender says. "He shoots."

I studied the face of the one with the shotgun, looking for mercy or hesitation. He had three tear drop tattoos under his dark eyes that were liquid with indifference. I thought of Brandy Redfern and the nephew named Charlie I hadn't met and how I minded the idea of dying for the first time in as long as I could remember. The shotgun pressed hard around my mouth, the smell of gun powder filling my nose and throat. My eyes began to water from the impact as my head slammed back against the wall. My left hand was led by the wrist above my shoulder and flat against the wall. The tool box opened and a drill whirred once.

"Now, Mister, this is how it going to go," the bartender said. "You're going to tell me what you know about this girl or we gonna get to work on you like we tearing down a house. Slowly."

The shotgun pulled back a few feet from my face.

"Like what?" I asked, my throat dry and desperate.

"Like who gave you this picture."

He flashed it for evidence and then flicked it across the room.

"It belongs to Dinny Tuite," I said with nothing to lose.

"I know that motherfucker," the bartender said, his face twisting into itself. "You seen him around?"

I shook my head.

"But you looking for him?"

I nodded.

"Why?"

"His boss hired me to find him."

"You a detective or some shit?"

"Sometimes."

"So, Mr. Detective, what'chu find out?"

I shook my head. "That he's gone is all I know."

The bartender said something in Spanish.

"This is how it going to be, Esse," the bartender said. "I think you holding out on me, that you know something you ain't sharing, that you lying about what you know about Dinny and the girl, so we going to hurt you until you tell me. Sound good? Oh, and if you make any noise or make any move, even close that hand, he's going to blast you in the face. Blowwww!"

I jerked from the exclamation and could smell sweat from under my clothes. My raised hands felt leaded; tension rippled across my shoulders and upper back. It was hard to breath as my lungs constricted and adrenalin whipped around my body. The drill whirred again, and I closed my eyes and waited for it to bore into my palm. But the motor weakened and sputtered to an impotent gurgle.

There was mumbling in Spanish and the sound of items shifting in the tool box. The pain arrived in dull, hard fashion across the entirety of my open palm. Mallet. Something emanated from inside me, like a squelch up my esophagus that died in my throat as the hurt radiated out from the smashed bones in my hand, the mutilated cartilage. It felt, for a moment, that blood would blurt from my fingertips. I blinked and breathed, gritted my teeth to focus on the pain.

Being the despised little brother of the thick and vicious Salvatore Stiles had a benefit: I could take a beating like no one I'd ever known. Pain didn't frighten me, didn't send off the alarms of adrenalin spurred by the survival instinct. I'd learned to recognize its effect on the body and brain, and to know it was what it was: a warning system. Pain comes and pain goes. Keep breathing and deal. Accept it even.

The hammer came a second time, and the pain increased as damaged bones were damaged further. The crunch was audible. I made no sound. The bartender screwed up his face; the shotgun quivered. Dude with the mallet looked at the bartender for instruction.

"Damn. You OK, Esse?" the bartender asked, a mix of fascination and disbelief on his face. "You, like, psycho or something?"

I didn't move, though sensors were erupting all over my body, and my brain scrambled to find a means of escape.

The floor creaked outside the door. The bartender stepped back and huffed, shook his head and bunched his lips in distaste. He said something in Spanish and backed toward the exit. The shotgun in front of me started to quiver, and the dude with the hammer stole a glance at the tarp on the bed.

When the bartender undid the lock and cracked the door, it exploded back in his face and shattered into pieces. The murderer with the shotgun turned his head and I severed his knee cap with my steel-toed boot, using more force than I imagined possible. He screamed and dropped the weapon. Bones walked in, picked up the sawed-off, and pointed it at the guy who dropped the mallet and held up his hands. I kicked that guy in the balls and watched him drop and writhe and groan on the ground next to his fallen partner. I took his arm back and snapped it with my boot at the elbow, the sound grotesque and satisfying. He screamed and keened and wailed.

I had my knife out of my boot as the bartender got to his feet. I ventilated his silk shirt with great speed and prejudice. I felt the knife separate his skin and drag across bone. It was sloppy work, and I was happy with it. Blood was starting to stain the starched burgundy and shredded surface when I turned away. As I picked the Polaroid up off the carpet, I heard his nose splatter when Bones bashed him in the face with the butt of the gun.

"I'm coming back to burn this place down," Bones said and made for the door. "Soon."

I followed him down the stairwell lit with Christmas lights that no longer seemed so magical. In the barroom, three near-naked women

were bound and gagged and fastened tightly to chairs. Flor had tears
pouring down her face, though a look of relief flashed in her eyes upon
seeing me alive.

I walked up to her with my good hand held up. She nodded
desperately in a manner that could be trusted. I could sense Bones
behind me, assuming the shotgun raised. I freed Flor's mouth from the
gag and showed her the picture.

"You know her?" I asked.

She nodded.

"What's her name?"

"Nathalia," she said in a barely audible voice.

"Nathalia what?"

"Valdez."

"She from around here?"

Flor nodded.

I held up my hand, reminding her of the promise not to move just
yet. She nodded the same nod as before. I cut her loose from the chair
and gave her the knife. She rubbed her wrists and thanked me with her
eyes.

"Wait two minutes, then cut them loose, and then get the fuck out of
here, OK?"

"Oh, hell yeah," she said, hugging her shoulders and shaking.

I made for the door on legs I could hardly feel. My hand began to
throb as the adrenalin wore off in the evening cool that felt like God's
breath blowing new skin on my worn body and tired life. I'd been close
to dying but never that close. Or maybe it was the fact that I wanted to
live more than ever before. Bones took out a handkerchief and wiped
down the handle of the shotgun, then he angled it against the stoop and
stomped it into dysfunction with a very large foot.

Street lights blinked on as we crossed the yard and got in the car.
Bones drove off at a casual clip. I held my damaged hand up and clasped
my wrist as if the pain could be cut off by a makeshift tourniquet.

"Thanks," I said.

Bones nodded and squinted dreamily, envisioning his return to torch that place. Lights flashed by as we got the fuck out of Mattison.

The pain in my hand became excruciating and waves of fatigue and fear blasted from behind my eyes, and I blinked hard to stay awake. I was startled awake by a big hand on my shoulder. We were in front of the emergency entrance to the hospital closest to my town. I walked out of Bones' car without a word.

Chapter 26

After some emergency room treatment that ended in a plaster cast from my knuckles to my elbow, a local cab company dropped me off behind the Inn, and I slipped up the backstairs to the office for a quick shower and change of clothes. A need to join the bustle below hastening my first attempts at life minus one appendage. I undressed, showered and dressed then ambled into the crowded Inn to find Richie as stressed as I'd ever seen him.

"The hell have you been?" he hissed in a tone that hinted at confidentiality until he noticed my condition. "Jesus fucking Christ. What happened to your hand, guy?"

"Slammed it in a door," I said.

He didn't believe me but made like he did.

"Listen," he said. "We're slammed here. Place is a madhouse. There's all sorts of rumors around town about Dinny Tuite not being dead but gone missing. Your pal Mike McBride's been in here four times and called just as many. Fuck is going on?"

"Long story," I said, ignoring the stares from bar patrons on my way to the kitchen, not sure how much help I could be with one good hand.

"And, oh," Richie called. "Some kid, claims to be your nephew, is in the dining room. Been waiting on you for, I dunno, about three hours now."

I turned around and Richie held up his hands to the sides, exasperated by a suddenly unreliable employer. I nodded in contrition and bee-lined through the waitress station that co-joined the two rooms.

It was crowded, waitresses and bus boys in a concert of ordering and delivering and clearing. Checks being paid. It was the kind of scene a restaurant owner should love, but none of it mattered in that moment. I searched the room, nearly frantic, until there he was, all alone in a booth by the frosted street side window, a kid in a gray t-shirt in front of a half-finished Root Beer Float. His hair was short and thick and brown, pushed up from his forehead in a small smack of defiance.

"And how are you, Charlie?" I asked, the words bouncing around my mouth as they were spoken.

He looked up, and I about died. There was a space between his front teeth and some Redfern in his rosy cheeks and green eyes, but his mother was right, this kid was a Stiles: the jaw line and hairline and aquiline nose. He was tall for his age and narrow in the shoulders and skinny in the arms like me and Angie were at 11 years old, but his frame was sure to bloom in the coming years. Curiosity bounced around his face and eyes as he blinked and fumbled for something to say until noticing my cast.

"What happened to your hand?" he asked with great concern for a man he'd never met before.

His voice was soft and sweet with a polite southern accent. I loved him already.

"It's nothing," I said. "You had enough to eat?"

"Yeah, I mean, yes," he said. "Mama brought me here before dinner to meet you, but when you weren't here she left me because they told her you'd be in soon and they couldn't leave me in the bar so they put me here and brought me a cheeseburger with French fries and the waitresses and everyone have been really nice, but I've been here so long, waiting."

"I'm sorry about that," I said as shame swept across my face and neck. "I really am."

"That's OK."

"And where is your mother?"

"Oh. She's in school. In college. She goes at night. Two days, I mean, two nights a week. I usually stay home or with Paw Paw in his nursing home, but tonight she brought me here to meet you. She says you're my uncle."

"I am," I said with what must have been something akin to pride. My insides pulsed and coursed with warmth.

I shook his hand. It felt moist and like a soft shell, the bones fragile. I wanted to protect them and not let go.

His eyes bloomed as he sat up. "Mama says your name is Caesar."

"It is."

"That's so cool."

"I guess."

"Can I call you Uncle Caesar?"

"If you'd like."

He smiled and so did I. It felt so nice.

"Why are you crying?" he asked.

"I'm sorry," I said, blotting tears on the shoulders of a fresh white T. I sniffed and tried to comport myself. "Long story."

"OK," he said. "Can you tell me?"

I sat down next to my nephew and told him all the good things I could remember about my beloved brother and his shining prince of a father. And then we just talked for a while. He was a good kid, and I was so happy to meet him.

Chapter 27

Charlie's mother found us in the kitchen where I was teaching him how to work a sauté pan. Being the only kid of a single parent, he had some culinary basics. He could make eggs, and that was great practice for a lot of dishes. He had helped Santi on a few plates, including a veal picatta that took a splash of white wine that flashed with sizzle and smoke and made him blurt "Cool!"

Brandy was tired and hungry when she arrived, and so was I, not having eaten since the roast beef sandwich courtesy of Ira Zeiler over eight hours earlier. Quite a bit had happened over that time.

The restaurant had only lingerers by then, so Santi went home. The bar was bumping with Friday night revelers after booze and company. Richie had that covered. With one hand, I put on a pot of water for pasta and coached Charlie through the dicing of pancetta and the slivering of a red onion. His mother cringed as he worked a large knife, but he was careful and a good listener. He sautéed the pancetta over medium heat, rendering out the fat, and then added the onions to caramelize in the drippings. I had him squish with his bare hand whole tomatoes and add them to the pan along with some torn basil which he thoughtfully sniffed before dropping.

As the sauce gently bubbled, Charlie salted the boiling water and added a pound of thick spaghetti with a hole in the middle. I taught him how to say "Bucatini." When the bucatini was three minutes shy of al dente, he strained it and dumped the strainer - wet noodles and all - right into the sauté pan where it finished cooking in the sauce, absorbing some of the flavor. I asked him not to tell anyone my secret for the most flavorful pasta, of pasta not just coated in sauce but of the sauce; and he promised he wouldn't. I believed him.

Using two hands, Charlie transferred the pasta and sauce from the massive sauté pan to a rounded platter, where he anointed it with fresh olive oil, added some grated Pecorino cheese and tossed the contents. Fresh basil was put on top as a garnish. His mother clapped, and Charlie beamed as his mother and his uncle enjoyed his creation at a makeshift table around a high wooden work station in the kitchen.

About half way through our plates, Mike, in uniform, came into the kitchen. He said a quick hi to Brandy, and I introduced him to my nephew, to whom he nodded somewhat coldly. I offered Mike some pasta, but he said no. And although he took a long look at my hand, he didn't ask what happened or where I'd been all day.

"Can I talk to you for a minute?" he said in a somewhat officious tone.

"Go ahead."

"Alone."

"I'm having my dinner," I said.

"It's kind of important."

"Not more important than my dinner. Charlie made it all by himself."

Mike huffed in exasperation, took a breath, and walked out of the kitchen.

"What was that all about?" Brandy asked.

"Got me," I said and looked at Charlie. "Guy clearly doesn't know the magnificence of a perfectly prepared bucatini."

He smiled, and I tussled his hair with my good hand. When we were finished, I suggested Charlie show his mother how well he could wash dishes.

"It's part of kitchen work," I said when he playfully turtled his head. Brandy looked pleased; she also suddenly looked more weary than tired.

"Everything all right?" I asked.

"Yeah," she said. "It's just something at school."

"What class?"

"English Composition."

"Well, maybe I can help you then," I suggested. "I never made it beyond the 9th grade, but I've read more literature than most college graduates, I figure. Not a bad writer, either."

It was true; the library was the sanctuary in every town or city I stayed. I also fancied myself a pretty good writer having sent my mother long, narrative dispatches from all over America, allowing her to see and taste and hear and feel every city and every town I was in. I was also the son of one of the world's best unknown, rebellious men of poems and letters.

"No thanks, baby," Brandy said with a tilted smile. "It's not that kind of trouble."

"Well, what kind of trouble is it then?" I asked, feeling protective.

Brandy sighed and felt the need to confess.

"The professor's kinda giving me a hard time, is all."

"About your work?"

"About other things, actually."

I remembered when one of Mike's big sisters, a real beauty, was at college and her being harassed by a professor to the point of her having to transfer. I also remembered that Mike's father, out of uniform, paid that inappropriate professor a visit.

"Maybe I should have a word with this professor of yours?"

Brandy looked bewildered and then bemused. "What did you just say?"

I was seeing more of the bewildered at that point, so I repeated my slightly veiled threat, thinking I was being noble.

"I'm sorry, but are you out of your damn mind?" Brandy said, ending any ambiguity in her stance.

Charlie stopped washing the dishes and approached us quickly. "Everything all right, Mama?"

"Everything's fine, Charlie, except your uncle seems to think I'm incapable of handling my own affairs."

"I didn't say that," I said, even though that's exactly what I said.

Brandy's eyes pulsed and her mouth opened as disbelief segued toward anger. The urge to engage in a heated exchange might have come over her, but she took a breath to calm herself and placed her hands slowly on her thighs. She looked around the kitchen and at her son and she was, I believe, considering how things had improved for them as of late. "I must have been mistaken then," she said, a thread of feigned contrition in her voice.

"You weren't mistaken," I said. "And I'm sorry."

Brandy Redfern broke out laughing, one of those big, bouncy laughs that actresses use in movies.

"You hear that, Charlie?" she asked with a whole new look, one of pleasant satisfaction.

"I did," he answered, nodding with a satisfied smile of his own.

"Heard what?" I asked, feeling suddenly outnumbered and excluded, realizing how much private knowledge they must share. I wanted in.

Brandy gave me the jackpot smile of warmth and genuine affection. "One of the rules for being a good man is being able to say you're sorry. Right, Charlie?"

"Right," he said and went back to the sink to finish the dishes.

I wondered what other rules they had about being a good man, and just how my life would measure up. I'd have a lot to apologize for, I imagined.

Chapter 28

I met Mike in the barroom after seeing Brandy and Charlie out with hugs and a promise to spend more time together the very next day. I would have been sleep walking by that point had I not been so high from my encounter with Charlie and the promise of a new family. I was basically a brother-in-law and a legitimate uncle. That kid had the same blood as me. We looked alike. I took it as a sign of the curse lifting or, at least, an opportunity to do something of purpose. Mike had other concerns than my tragic family history and unremarkable life to that point; he only wanted to pursue shit that mattered to him: the results of my unconventional investigation over the course of a very long day.

"We gotta go back," he said.

"Back to where?"

"To the whore house," he said as if I was daft. "The girl is missing, too, clearly. They must have taken off together. Maybe someone there knows something. Maybe that skank you let loose."

I'd had told him, over a beveled low ball of Balvenie, about what happened that day, about Ira Zeiler, and Cha Cha Porter, and my odyssey with Bones that nearly led to my shotgun funeral with a tarp for a casket. I raised my busted hand as hard evidence of good fortune and a lesson learned.

What I didn't tell him was how bent I was over his indifference to my nephew sitting in my kitchen. He knew Angie as well as anyone, and he knew my history of a broken family and what any sign of redemption might have meant to me, but he cared more about a missing person's case and about some married girl he was fucking right in front of her husband's eyes. His privilege of a stable family and a stable childhood and a fledgling career as a civil servant turned the mellow scotch bitter in my mouth. Empathy was not for the entitled, I gathered. At least not when your own competing interests were involved.

"You go," I said. "I'm done with this shit."

"What?" Mike asked, incredulous. "You can't do that. Dick Donaghy gave you ten grand."

"I'm pretty sure, at this point, we're fucking even," I said, once again, raising my hand and fighting the exasperation that crawled up my throat. "Besides, he can rest his head at night knowing that he and his precious daughter will never see the likes of Dinny Tuite again."

"What do you got against the Donaghy's, Caes?" Mike asked, puzzled by the push back. "They're good people. Town's people. And they haven't done anything to you."

"I can't speak for the daughter, though I hear she's got shit taste in men," I said, unable to avoid the silent shot at my oldest friend who was all over my nerves. "But the father is a fucking asshole who made it his job to make Dinny Tuite miserable just because he didn't like his kind."

"And what kind is that?"

"Let's call him different and leave it at that since that's enough for Dick Donaghy types."

Mike huffed some air out of his nose as if I couldn't possibly understand the entitlements obliged to the good families of the world. He helped himself to more of my scotch, incriminated by silence as I put the bottle back on the shelf and began to shut the joint down.

That's the problem I had with small towns: the small minds and group think and xenophobia that makes people intolerant and suspicious of others, even if they're from the other side of somewhere nearby. I'd experienced this as a kid from the other side of the tracks and much more of this on the road as a perpetual stranger, and especially

ANDREW COTTO

when I toured the Delta with the bluesman Macie Turner. People looked with immediate resistance, if not outright scorn, upon the odd duo of the giant black man with gray corn rows and his olive sidekick with the long brown hair. We were others, and that was enough to make us less. People could be fucking idiots. And I wasn't about to be any part of that. I shut the joint down and ushered Mike out, not giving a shit if and when I'd see him again. And not thrilled overall about the ways of man.

Chapter 29

Weeks went by and leaves fell from the majestic trees in town and Charlie became a fixture at the Inn on nights when his mother went to school and on weekends. He did the dishes and helped Santi work the line. I taught him knife and pan skills; how to trim loins of filet and pound veal into tenderness; how to dice fruit he'd deliver to Richie at the bar who called him "Kid." Charlie told me that he missed Florida and that the kids at his new school picked on him for talking different and for dressing funny. He had no friends and nowhere to ride his BMX bike. His mother wouldn't let him out of the apartment building on his own, and he didn't blame her because the streets around there were kind of scary. He brought his skateboard to the Inn on weekends and pushed it around town much of the day. There was even a skate park now, in the area of town by the baseball fields and playground. He started meeting up with two kids named Kenny and Brian. I told him to bring them in any time for hamburgers and ice cream sundaes. We'd make them his signature pasta, too.

The local authorities declared Dinny Tuite dead in the middle of October though no trace of him was ever found. They claimed he, like two others unaccounted for, must have been in the wreckage up front eviscerated by the explosion. I suspected otherwise - as the other two were conductors, front and center of the action - but I kept that theory to myself. My hand was healing, and I wanted to put all that Dinny Tuite business behind me.

After an absence of a week or so, after our disagreement of sorts, Mike started coming into the bar on a regular basis like nothing had ever happened. It was like that when we were kids - we'd get into a fight over something or other, avoid each other for a few days, and then just pick up without a word. I was still bothered by his involvement in all this, his secrets and subtle manipulation, his self-interest above all else, though I never mentioned I knew about him and Katie Donaghy or asked about his aspirations with the FBI, and I was glad I hadn't told him the name of Nathalia Valdez. I hoped her and Dinny Tuite were happy somewhere.

Once my hand healed, I joined Mike's gym and we worked out together three mornings a week, and he began to teach me this new combination of martial arts and boxing that I enjoyed very much. The exertion and the contact cleared my head and lungs and strengthened my body. I needed the mental release, and there was only so much I could accomplish with steel-toes to the knees and being good with a knife. I hoped that violence was behind me - in this moment of life that felt so fresh and new - but I wasn't a fool any more than I was a saint.

The days started to pass in a fluid motion, and a sense of routine was established that had me, for the first time in my life, feeling something akin to content. I spent a lot of time with Charlie and hung out in the barroom with a regular crowd of men and women about my age after the kitchen closed. I started making meatballs and manicotti on Sundays, mounds of ziti and baked chicken, too, like my mother used to do, and a regular crowd would come in that almost felt like family; they even convinced me to get a TV in the barroom so they could watch the New York Giants play football, though they couldn't yet convince me to join their co-ed softball team.

Brandy rekindled some friendships from high school and her crew met at the Inn on Sundays, too. Charlie palled around with a few of their kids. Santi and Junior came in after church with their extended families; their kids mixing it up with Charlie and company; their wives insisting on helping me in the kitchen and with clean up.

It was all pastoral and good until I stepped out back for a late night smoke on a cool Sunday in early November and found Tommy Funk knocked out cold with a note from my father duct taped to his face.

Chapter 30

And how are you, my son?

A man could stay busy watching your back door. I found this sneaky fucker looking antsy and malevolent outside of your fine establishment. And not the first time I'd seen him either. He reminded me of the juvenile delinquents I suggested you avoid while growing up. So I removed him of his weapon of death (now disposed) and put him to rest for a while with a spell I learned from an IRA man out of Limerick who recommends a blow to the back of the head with a blunt object. Not as subtle as a curse, but effective nonetheless.

I'm not the murderous type, now, and neither do I suspect are you, but I do suggest you find a way to remove this cancer from your midst. And then we can have a conversation about our family.

Bye now son,

Your Father, Timothy Stiles

I was a fool for letting my guard down and embarrassed to need a watchdog, but I was also grateful to be under the watchful eye of my estranged father. I had to figure out what to do with Tommy Funk. His agenda seemed larger than some tinny revenge on Sallie's behalf; the threat far more legitimate. It had to be connected to the blackmail of Cha

Cha Porter, with stupid Tommy there thinking I could be a complication. Maybe he was trying to kill me outside the AC that night. That didn't seem possible. Too public and pathetically executed. Something must have altered his attitude toward me. Convinced him that a gun was appropriate. I considered the possibilities, and it suddenly made sense.

It was the desperation of being the outsider, scorned in your own surroundings. The deplorable types, looked down upon by the better-offs, of whom you had to hate in return in order to maintain some semblance of dignity. It was the source of much of the awfulness out in the world: Us vs Them, with "Us" always being in the right. I knew the feeling. And I knew where it was coming from now.

I threw Tommy Funk over my shoulder and carried him across the street to Huey's lot and tossed him in the large dumpster aside the garage, hoping that Huey himself would get the message and get out of town before Cha Cha Porter came calling. The next morning, I took the bus to Bayonne to tell what I knew to Cha Cha Porter, and I ended up, a short while later, on a private plane leaving the country.

Chapter 31

Cha Cha Porter was happy to see me, and even happier to get the name and whereabouts of his amateur extortionist. It made sense. Sallie must have shared his shit on Cha Cha Porter with Tommy Funk. And Tommy must have passed it on to Huey, who saw it as a shot to make some money. The town where he had lived his whole life no longer seemed like home to him. He fixed the cars of people who were better than him. He hung around the AC with the dregs of town, like Tommy Funk. No wonder Huey looked so defeated, turning into mush. Still, I was a little insulted that he'd go so far as to see me killed. I always thought he liked me.

I wasn't so offended by Huey's murderous intentions to enact upon him the same fate. When Cha Cha Porter asked if his men should put the fear of God in Huey or actually deliver him to God, I suggested they go with the former. Same for Tommy Funk. Once those lightweights got the sense of the power they were fucking with, they'd surely make amends and disappear without a trace. I also didn't want a double homicide in my town. Bad for business and the general mood of which I was now invested personally and financially.

Cha Cha sent Bones and Fat Elvis to pay a visit to my town after they dropped me and their boss off at Teterboro Airport, a small air field dedicated to charter flights. We boarded a small jet with a two-man crew and no attendants. The cabin was carpeted and comfortable enough; Cha Cha and I sat in opposing lounge chairs over a coffee table strewn with luxury travel magazines and important journals which we didn't read. He told me how he found Nathalia Valdez.

Bones had shared the story of our escape from the brothel. They knew of the establishment already, it had been there for years, but they weren't aware of its recent fall into the hands of a street gang out of El Salvador that had, somehow quietly, taken over the vice rings in Mattison. Cha Cha laughed and said I was lucky to be alive. I didn't find it all that funny, but his point was well-taken. I had gotten in way over my head.

Bones had also overheard the name of the girl in the Polaroid and thought to share with Cha Cha who found out through a contact at the Port Authority that she had been on a flight out of Newark Airport to Santo Domingo, Dominican Republic, night of the train explosion, accompanied by a David McCarthy.

"And who is that?" I asked.

"That's not the dude you looking for?"

"Nope."

"Sheeet," Cha Cha laughed. "Dude is smart. Got himself an alias. Get the fuck out of town without leaving a trace."

That's what I was now figuring, too. Dinny Tuite and Nathalia Valdez met at one of the skin joints in Mattison, where he would spend his afternoons after cutting out of work (post lunch buffet, if he were me). Miserable as a motherfucker in the trappings of American suburbia, being a city kid with an urban style, in a small town full of small minds, married to the wrong woman, son-in-law to a son-of-a-bitch, Dinny fell for a woman who, like him, existed in the periphery of society. He didn't care if she stripped or humped for money. They were going to run away together. The plan must have been in the works, and Dinny, smart as he supposedly is, got the idea to bolt when the explosion happened as it would give him a few days, if a not a few weeks, cover.

But even the smartest can suffer from bad luck sometimes, and it was bad luck for Dinny Tuite that I ended up on his case at the same time one of my brother's debtors came calling. So now it was Dinny Tuite versus me and Cha Cha Porter. He had a lot more to fear in Cha Cha than me; at best, me and Dinny Tuite were a fair fight in both strength and cunning, but Cha Cha Porter was a force of nature, a man two steps ahead of law enforcement and a country mile ahead of the likes of me, evidenced by the fact that I found myself sequestered with him on a flight bound for the Dominican Republic for reasons having absolutely nothing to do with him.

"Can I ask you something?"

"Why not?" he answered.

He flicked some lint off the front of his red Guayabera shirt and laced his fingers before his chest.

"Why are you helping me here?" I asked.

He unlaced his fingers and leaned over the table, looked both ways and then at me, his eyes wide and cold as ceramic plates. "Isn't that the type a question you supposed to ask *before* you get on a private plane, destination unknown, in the company of a professional criminal?"

"Hadn't thought of that," I answered, my mouth turning dry.

"Man has to know his limitations," he said, leaning back into his leather chair. "People get hurt, caught, all sorts of bad shit, when they overplay their hand."

I told Cha Cha Porter about the two martini rule. He liked it, laughed and then answered my original question. It involved money laundering through the Inn. I resisted at first, despite the decent chunk of money promised monthly for little to no work and even less risk. I trusted Cha Cha's smarts and knew that business with him - at least on that level - would be as safe as could be expected. I was hung up on the bigger picture.

"Sheeet," Cha Cha drawled with a little Latin accent on the finish. "Didn't have you pinned as a choir boy."

I assured him I was not.

"But you have a soul, right?"

I told him I did.

"As do I," he said.

I agreed.

"Let me tell you something," he said, his eyes drawn closer together. "There is corruption, in some respect, in nearly every facet of society, from Little League to law enforcement, to the highest levels of government. You understand?"

I did.

"Hell," he guffawed without mirth. "As we speak, a Catholic priest somewhere is fondling the genitalia of an Alter boy, if you're looking for any definitive proof of the notion."

I waited for the point in the din of the engine hum with clouds floating by the port hole windows above the wet bar.

"I was involved in law enforcement for many years, had a nice career ahead of me. Then I got on the wrong side of someone important, too much in their dirty business, got my ass bumped to the prison system. And let me tell you something, what we do to the incarcerated in this country is a crime against humanity. I saw it first hand and immediately regretted ever putting even the most hardened criminal behind bars." He crossed his arms and continued. "So what I began doing is providing them some humanity. You know, the kind of treatment white collar criminals get while imprisoned. Access to women and quality drugs; the kind of food that made Fat Anthony who he is today."

We shared a laugh.

"Make you a drink?" I asked.

"Don't disappoint," he answered with a sly turn of his head.

The small wet bar was stocked with mostly mediocre liquors but a top shelf bourbon and some bitters, so while I whipped us up a couple of Old Fashioneds, minus the garnish but including sugar snatched from the coffee station, Cha Cha told me how his lucrative and humanitarian effort (the latter term accompanied by a well-timed wink as I placed the drink in front of him) inspired such effort on the outside as well, where he provided what he called "clean vice" in such a successful manner it inspired his retirement from the prison system, full pension in place, and the purchase of a number of legit establishments to launder the profits. He needed a new place, though, now that Glory Social was on the radar of the FBI.

"Are you in?" he asked.

I thought of Brandy and Charlie Redfern, and the things I'd be willing to do to keep them safe and secure. "I am," I said. "If we find Dinny Tuite."

"Oh, we will," he said with the confidence of a great man.

Cha Cha Porter and I clinked glasses. My cocktail did not disappoint. We sipped our drinks in silence for a few minutes.

"How do you think Sallie became an informant?" I asked casually to belie my serious interest.

"That I do not know," he said. "Been bothering me, since we had that place locked down good, from the warden on down. We had a zero rat population and with good reason. So how anyone, and particularly someone such as your brother, no offense..."

"None taken."

"...but him being connected to the Feds is a stone-cold mystery to me." Cha Cha Porter sipped his drink and then looked at me hard. "How would the federal government of these here United States, in a million years, identify Salvatore Stiles, of all people, as a potential informant? You have any idea?"

"No," I lied.

Chapter 32

The plane touched down at a small airport on the northern coast of the island. Upon approach, the water, in disparate shades of blue, looked surreal out beyond the craggy shoreline and extending into infinity. I'd never been to the Caribbean or any such place of blue, blue water. I'd never been out of the country except, figuratively speaking, for some time spent in the Bayou of Louisiana working at a roadhouse outside of Lafayette inhabited by people who didn't consider themselves American but Cajun or Creole instead.

The air was hot and dusty. The sun, behind a thin layer of clouds, a smoldering pearl. A black car awaited with a driver who proceeded down a pot-holed track lined with scrub brush and palm trees, marked by flattened iguanas. The car was not so new and over air conditioned, the third-world suspension system taking every bump. A phone was built into a console between the seats in back, and Cha Cha rested his arm on it as we bounced along.

"How far is Santo Domingo?" I asked.

"About four hours," Cha Cha said.

"There wasn't a closer airport?"

"This look like an international airport to you?"

"Wouldn't know," I said. "First time flying."

"No shit?"

"None."

"Damn, man," Cha Cha said. "You a mother fucking enigma wrapped up in a mystery and a whole lot of denim."

I was already feeling uncomfortable and out of sorts, dressed as I was for late autumn in New Jersey in jeans and a jean jacket over a white thermal, big black boots. Cha Cha said something in Spanish to the driver who nodded.

"We'll make a stop on the way," Cha Cha assured me.

"Sounds good," I said. "On the way where?"

"You'll see," he said. "Got a hunch."

Cha Cha began to work the phone as I stared out the window and wondered where we could be going as the road split small villages of colorful and crumbling abodes, faded storefronts; Coca-Cola signs. The streets were spotted with nut-colored elders in old clothes. Shoeless children chased each other with sticks and threw balls against walls. Wild dogs roamed. Chickens crossed the road. Women in long, tight cotton skirts glided along, ignoring the comments from men passing on motor bikes or on foot. Past the villages, guarded compounds grew out of the shoreline with majestic hotels yawning to the skyline.

We stopped in a small town of sorts that functioned as an outdoor shopping mall, with high-end international brands in a row of colorful storefronts stretched along a single boulevard walking distance from the resorts. There were lots of military police armed with automatic weapons on the streets and very few locals. In one of the more casual stores, Cha Cha tried to talk me into shorts and sandals, but the best he could do was to get me to swap my jean jacket and thermal for a lightweight, short sleeve button down stitched with tiny palm trees. I thought I looked pretty good, and even better when paired with a straw Borsalino hat. From a street stand, I bought Brandy a necklace of small seashells and Charlie a bracelet of twine that would shrink around his wrist after getting wet.

I could feel my olive skin turn in the hard sun as Cha Cha and I walked away from the tourist area and turned down a back alley to grab some lunch at a bodega with a cafe set up in the back. We sat at a card table and Cha Cha flirted with an ageless and smiling waitress with a plunging neckline and heart-shaped ass. She brought us fried root vegetables and slow-roasted pork with rice and beans that we washed down with local beer in green bottles.

"So," Cha Cha said after wiping his mouth with a coarse paper napkin. "What chu going to do when you find this gentleman?"

I liked how his accent came out when on native turf.

"Dunno," I said.

"Better start thinking," Cha Cha said, signaling the waitress for the check. "We'll be there soon."

"Be where?"

"There."

Chapter 33

Cha Cha's phone calls confirmed his hunch. And we were destined for an unfettered string of towns along the coast that were off the general tourist radar and even unknown to most Dominican nationals. It was a sophisticated and secret exile for many of history's outlaws: Nazis, mobsters, despots, oligarchs, warlords, celebrities, union leaders, politicians. And, of course, white collar figures who gamed the system and then split. Cha Cha said that these days it was mostly a retirement spot for Europeans looking to live in luxury where their currency went far, but it was still known as a place to not be known.

I used the car phone to call Richie back in the States. I didn't tell him I was down in the Dominican Republic closing in on Dinny Tuite with the help and company of a notorious and nearly untouchable crime boss. I did tell him that I wouldn't be in that night and asked for him to open and to have Santi close. He didn't ask where I was, but his tone suggested suspicion and even a little concern.

"Take care of yourself, all right?" he said before hanging up.

Good advice. Charlie wasn't due in that night, but he was on my mind as I tried to figure out what to do if I had Dinny Tuite in hand. I was kind of on his side. He probably thought he had accomplished the American Dream, rising up from the inner city through the public education system, getting a scholarship to a top-notch college, meeting a beautiful co-ed, marrying her and moving to her bucolic town near a major city where you could get rich and be happy. But what he didn't know was that the town, or - at least - the part he married into, didn't want him around.

I thought of Dinny Tuite as black Irish, but Richie implied, with a casual and sinister racism, that he was more black than Irish. I guess that toxic implication applied to anyone in this country who doesn't fit the mainstream American archetype: white, well-off, of traditional values, and a traditional manner of speaking and behaving. No exceptions. In or out. With us or against us. The ways of man.

That's why Dinny Tuite reminded me of my father; they both possessed immense talents and had a way about them that some - but not enough - found charming. So they were kept out on the fringes, where the unwanted and the denied lived their lives. And while some preferred it out there, beyond the mainstream, there was still a sense of bitterness toward those who deemed you not good enough based on terms that were not fair or just not your own. I knew how they felt. I had started to think that I didn't belong out there on the periphery; but now I had my doubts.

Cha Cha Porter stared out the window at the ocean beyond a desolate stretch of cracked prairie spotted with scrub brush and thicket under a blanket of blue, blue sky. He occasionally checked the fledgling spots on the back of his hand like a man might glance at his watch, not really checking the time. The spot below his lower lip had grown larger since we'd first met, and I wondered how much time he spent worrying about such a glaring assault on his appearance. My sense (and my hope) was that he was bothered by it but too sure of himself, too burnished by life and triumphant over its adversity, to be overly concerned with superficial things. Quite an accomplishment.

The town reminded me of a larger, fancier version of European villages in Hemingway stories, of pastel facades and wooden porticos around a town square of dirt that was hosed down in the morning and evening, where people drank cold beer under verandas. The type of town that sacrifices its modest elegance a few times a year for festivals. The square here was broad and of cobblestone. A large fountain gurgled in the center, and statues of men on horses guarded the four corners. The storefronts were active with a mix of well-dressed, sun-kissed people walking slowly. There was an aura of exclusivity. I doubted if they had festivals. People in swimwear rode bicycles with baskets up front on a small path toward the shoreline where waves clapped and shredded on the stone jetties. White birds circled above the water's edge, and the sound of their screeches carried on the air that was cool and fragrant, of salt and wild herbs and a sense of privileged privacy.

The car had stopped outside the square and idled as Cha Cha went off on a fact-finding mission. He returned 15 minutes later, licking an ice cream cone and smiling like the world worked for him.

"There's a young gringo and even younger Latina got here last month," he reported with a daft air. "Out practically every night on the town."

I rubbed my chin.

"Think that might be them?" Cha Cha asked, his eyes wide in mock ignorance.

"Just might be," I said, enjoying his company. "Any idea where to find them?"

"Shouldn't be too hard," he said, now serious. "Let's get clean, grab some supper, and tear this town up."

Chapter 34

Cha Cha checked into a boutique hotel and offered to get me a room, but I declined and went for a walk in the shaded loggia around the circumference of the square. The shops were international, mostly European with lots of French and Italian presence. None of the clothes, watches, bags, shoes, or whatnot, interested me at all. I had a hard time imagining people paying such prices for these things. I was happy to have been spared the impulses of consumerism, my new shirt and hat aside.

The cafes were sleek and well-lit; I took a strong cup of coffee at a small bakery and treated myself to a rare encounter with a newspaper. I'd avoided the news through much of my adult life, only keeping up with what I heard tangentially or saw on the occasional news broadcast in a storefront window. I'd never owned a TV and only turned the one on in the bar for football games. My reading was dedicated almost entirely to literature, though a solid immersion in a reputable newspaper once in a while kept me tethered to reality just enough to have a sense of how things were with the world. An International Herald Tribune was on a table, so I picked it up and read it cover to cover.

The new American president seemed like a dangerous character. Smart but not as smart as he thought - brilliant and cunning, kind of like Cha Cha Porter, whose hubris, though, led the new president into public life. I'd heard a lot about Bill Clinton, his charm and his depravity, when he was governor of Arkansas and I was travelling around the Delta. It was clear people in power were out to get him, and I wondered how that would play out. His wife, and her ambition, seemed almost like more of a threat to the American standard than her husband's political skills and appeal to young people. Despite their privilege, they had that outsider thing going.

I met Cha Cha back in the hotel's foyer, a grand and fragrant room with comfortable chairs and potted flowers and cooled air. Cha Cha had on fresh clothes with a hand gun tucked into the waist band by the small of his back. We walked out into the comfortable night and the breeze lifted my hair of the shoulders of my new shirt. The square was quiet, and I followed Cha Cha without a word beyond the center of town to a small district full of lights and sound. Antique convertibles slow rolled down the wide boulevard. People of mixed races were dressed in colorful clothes. The mood was ebullient, and it reminded me of the Jazz age. We poked in and out of joints, staying only long enough to have a drink and scout the room for Dinny Tuite and Nathalia Valdez.

At the counter of a greasy spoon, we ate hamburgers in what I assumed was a respite from our search. When finished, Cha Cha led me through the kitchen and to a door manned by a muscle-bound bouncer on a stool. Cha Cha spoke to him quietly in Spanish, and then nodded at me with great expectation.

"Here we go," he said. "Our eagle has landed, and he right through this here door."

The door opened and past the mighty bouncer was a second door that opened to a warehouse space converted into a bustling supper club with people eating and drinking and smoking. Red, plush booths were spaced around the lower level and on the balcony that overlooked a dance floor moving to a live band that played Bachata. And there, in perfect rhythm with each other, practiced and uninhibited, right in the middle of the floor, was Dinny Tuite and Nathalia Valdez. She was a head shorter than her partner and more stunning with her clothes on, a low-cut canary blouse and flowing, patterned skirt that spun with each turn. He looked tan and sharp in a tight, beige T and pleated navy trousers, his hair slicked back.

Cha Cha stayed by the door, and I went to the long bar and watched them dance. I was reminded of my Carmen from Louisiana with cork screw hair and green apple eyes who taught me to Cajun jitterbug in her family's roadhouse outside of Lafayette. I missed dancing with her so very much, and often dreamed of just that, and I certainly wasn't planning to interrupt two lovers in an act of intimacy. Carmen used to joke that I liked eating and drinking more than sex, and she might have been kind of right about that; but she could also put dancing in that mix as well as it was far more romantic than mashing bodies together.

The handsome escape artists didn't stop dancing until the band took a break. When they returned to their table, a C-shaped booth on the far side of the dance floor, I sent over a pitcher of martinis and three glasses. When the waitress put the alcohol accoutrement on the table, Nathalia questioned her in harsh Spanish. I assumed it had to do with the origins of the drinks, and the three turned their heads in unison towards the spot at the bar where I had ordered, but I was at the waitress' side by then.

"And how are you?" I asked Dinny Tuite, taking off my hat.

The waitress left, and Dinny Tuite considered me as if an apparition. He turned his head. His mouth opened. Then closed. He ran a finger down the glistening pitcher of vodka and looked at the three glasses. His finger went up as the lightbulb of recognition went off. He stared hard into my eyes.

"The two martini guy," he said. "The runaway from shit town."

I nodded and put my hat on the table. His giant Adam's apple bobbed.

"What are you, on vacation or something?" he asked, suspicion increasing with each word.

"No," I said. "I don't take vacations."

"I'm sorry," Nathalia Valdez said without a hint of apology. "But do we know you?"

She spoke hard and fast and had a wounded air about her that suggested a capacity for great anger.

"You're from Mattison, right?" I asked her.

"So fucking what? Who in the fuck are you?"

"You've heard of Cha Cha Porter, right?"

"Of course I have," she said. "So fucking what?"

"He's over there, by the door," I said and raised a hand to Cha Cha. He nodded and lit a thin cigar.

"There's no getting past him," I said.

"Oh my fucking God," Nathalia said in what seemed like one long word. "The fuck in the hell is happening here?"

"Mind if I sit down?" I asked.

Dinny Tuite slid over to Nathalia's side of the booth and hooked his arm around the back of her neck. I poured out three martinis, though I was the only one who took a sip.

"I know what you're thinking," Dinny said to me.

I didn't respond.

"How could a guy run away from the perfect blondie wife and the perfect town," he said as if he had me all figured out. "The so-called American dream. Ain't that right?"

I knew the American dream was a farce, and I hadn't made up my mind about the town, but I had no preference for blondes; I liked independent women, who - more often than not - tended to be of color, but that was of no matter.

"Here's the deal," I said to Dinny. "Your wife's family hired me to find you."

He bunched up his mouth into an angry rosebud and breathed through his nose. He shook his head as if none of this made sense. How could he have been caught so easily? And by the runaway who fixed up the Inn. Nathalia rubbed his thigh and tried to soothe the coiling inside that called for fight or flight but knew neither was an option.

"I'll pay you more to not find me," he said with a now cool countenance. "Name your price."

"The good news," I said, ignoring his offer, "is that I think the Donaghy's are a bunch of fucking assholes, well, at least the father. He's the only one I've personally met. And from what I know, he's the only one who suspects that you're not dead."

Dinny creased a smile and agreed with a shake of his head. I imagine Katie Donaghy's old man gave him a real hard time, just objecting on so many levels to the reality of Dinny Tuite as his son-in-law. He also probably resented his great success and what it portended about the world. The din of the room picked up. Something broke into pieces somewhere. Dinners of steak and seafood were being served. It smelled of smoke and oranges and seared flesh. I sipped some of the martini and let the numbness spread over my lips.

"So what are you saying here?" Dinny asked. "That you're gonna do me a solid. Forget the whole thing cause you can't stand Dick Donaghy either? You came all the way down here to tell me that?"

Nathalia's brown eyes blossomed, and she looked innocent and devoid of all the injury she must have suffered before finding redemption in the love of Dinny Tuite. Of all of us outsiders at the table, she had the least agency over her life.

"What they want is the money, Dinny," I told him.

"Fuck that," he said. "I earned that shit. I never had none, and now I got some. I ain't giving that up. They got plenty of they own."

"I'm not sure that's the point," I said.

Dinny huffed. "It's funny," Dinny said. "That guy had this pipe up his ass about me from jump street, and he was with it non-stop. The way I talk and walk and everything. You know what I'm saying? I used to try to explain to him how I grew up, on the streets, that most of my friends were black, that I didn't have no father and my mother was a mental case, so I was in and out of foster homes, too, mostly with families of black folks, and I just grew up with them like family, and acting like them somewhat, so I just prefer people of color, you know? They raised me up and treated me right. I get them, and they get me. So, that makes me a little different. I know that, but that was my surroundings. Where I come from. And I don't try to change that shit for nobody. I think that's what Katie liked about me, man, that I wasn't like all those same old same old motherfuckers she dated in high school that looked a lot like the same old motherfuckers at Fordham. Clean cut, boring-ass, white dudes. She was on me like white on rice freshman year. I was surprised, for real. I went to a boarding school on scholarship my last couple years of high school, and them privileged white girls there wanted nothing whatsoever to do with me. The dudes were all like, 'Why you act black, man?' But Katie just seemed down with it. She used to tell me about where she grew up, and it sounded nice. You know what I'm saying? Quiet streets and nice houses and shit, but it wasn't all that nice when I got there. Those people in that town are fucking cold. Her friends and shit. A couple of her sisters and her sisters' husbands. And, of course, the father. They acted like I deuced in the punch bowl, man. That I had no right marrying their darling. Maybe they were right."

Dinny looked at Nathalia, who pulsed her eyes and fought off the anger pulsing beneath her skin. Dinny gave her a warm smile and gently kissed her forehead. It was quite beautiful, and the intimacy embarrassed me. I wish I'd left them alone, but I couldn't.

"What about Katie?" I asked.

"Thas' the thing, man," he said. "I ain't got no beef with Katie. I mean, yeah, we probably shouldn't of got married. Not maybe, for sure," he said, hooking his arm defiantly around Nathalia again. "I got ahead of myself on that one. Part of me just did it out of spite or ambition, and that was fucked up. I know that now. We rushed into it, but she's all right. She's cool. You know? School teacher and shit. Working with kids. But deep down, I know, she was more of a symbol to me. You know? Like the kind of life I thought that I wanted, but I was wrong. American dream and shit, but that world don't want cats like me. And fuck them. I don't want their bitch asses neither."

"Why not just get divorced?" I asked.

Dinny cringed and Nathalia gave him a look of severe inquiry with mouth flattened, nostrils flared, and brows raised. I guessed that this wasn't the first time the divorce conversation had come up.

"Look, man," Dinny said, shaking his head and giving Nathalia a quick glance. "I know this sounds whack, but her old man wouldn't let us. Behind all that jerk ass attitude, motherfucker is a serious Catholic. Church every morning before work kinda shit. Saturday nights and Sunday morning. No booze. No meat on Friday. Said he'd disown any of his kids if they ever got divorced, so Katie and I been living like we divorced for years, separate rooms and all that. But we cool with each other, and I've been thinking of a way out, and when that train shit went down, that was it."

"Were you even on the train?" I asked.

"Hell no, man. I was with this one, at her house. I heard about it on the news, and we was at the airport that night. *Hasta la vista* kinda shit."

"And it was all working out perfectly."

"Damn skippy."

Dinny leaned back and tilted up his chin. He and Nathalia looked so happy in that moment. I would have liked to take their picture, but I wasn't there to toast their success.

"And it was all well and good until I got here," I said.

"Yeah, motherfucker," Dinny said, removing his arm from around Nathalia's neck and leaning forward on the table, rattling the martini glasses. "I knew there was going to be some shit of some kind with you. Only dude around that town with half a brain, though I still don't know why you went back to that place."

I nodded knowingly at his recurring thought. "You've mentioned that, once or twice."

"Yeah, well, I sure as hell wish you hadn't come back," he said with a huff.

I sipped some martini and let that realization drift into the ether of the clamorous room.

"The fuck we do now?" Dinny asked. "You going to bring us back to New Jersey or some shit?"

"You're going to get me the hundred grand Dick Donaghy promised for finding you, so I can tell him that I didn't find you. And then you're going to figure out a way to get Katie Donaghy the kind of money she would get in a fair divorce, without her father finding out."

"And how the fuck am I gonna do that?"

"From what I understand, you're a very smart man. Figure something out."

Dinny Tuite grabbed the martini glass with a full fist by the thin stem, and I thought it would snap before reaching his lips. He took a big sip and stared at the end of his nose like a defeated boxer. He was considering the possibilities; I liked that.

The three of us sipped our drinks in silence for a while. Cha Cha Porter, now at the bar, talked to a statuesque and dark woman in a bright red dress. Nathalia Valdez crossed one leg over the other and looked over the room, worry working its way into the soft area around her eyes. I wanted to ask her to teach me their dance, but she didn't seem to be in the mood. We drank for a while in silence and were sitting on two martinis, thinking about a third, when Dinny looked up.

"Solid," he said. "I got it."

A big happy grin split his sharp and handsome face. He told me his plan. Dude was smart.

Chapter 35

A few weeks later I was sitting in Mike McBride's sedan, safely down the block from the Mattison bordello where I'd recently come close to dying. It was just after midnight on a Saturday, and I had cut out of the Inn early, leaving Richie in charge. It was cold out. Through the spines of leafless trees, the sky was jet black and rung with stars. The parking lot was nearly full behind the bordello, and it was still standing after I had asked Cha Cha to keep Bones from burning the joint down. Just for now.

In the Dominican Republic, on the way back to the airport, I'd picked up a bottle of premium rum for Bones and a new gold chain for Fat Elvis. And with my new standing with Cha Cha and his crew, I was able to drop a dime to Mike on the murderous gang out of Mattison trucking in heavy vice. It pleased me that Mike wasn't as clean cut as he made himself out to be, though I still had to confront his role as it pertained to me and mine.

"Let me ask you something?" I said as we sat in his silent sedan.

"Shoot, Caes," he said and lifted a set of small binoculars for what had to be the tenth time in the 20 minutes since we parked.

"You the one who connected Sallie with the FBI?"

Mike put the binoculars down and smiled without mirth.

"What makes you say that?"

"I didn't say that," I said. "I asked that."

"OK," he said with a small breath. "When I got back home from LA I learned pretty soon that Sallie was at Northern. I knew they were having a hard time finding informants and that the FBI had a hard on for Cha

Cha Porter, so I thought Sallie might be the man for the job. So, yeah, I suggested the meet, and that was all I knew until I saw him walking around town as a free man last spring."

"Did he see you?"

"I don't believe so."

"Yeah, I guess he would of mentioned it."

"Or not," Mike said with a true smile.

I laughed. Mike picked up the binoculars again.

"How about Katie Donaghy?"

Mike put down the binoculars and blushed. I was enjoying this: asking him questions at the wrong time and making him uncomfortable in his own skin right in front of my face.

"What about her?"

"How long have you been banging her?"

"Bang's a tough term, Caes."

"You're right," I said. "How long have you been sleeping with someone else's wife?"

Mike sucked his teeth and shook his head, coming to grips with the fact that I had the upper hand over him not just at that moment but in life in general. Cop work out in the ganglands of LA was tough work, but it was no match for a dozen years on your own in America.

"You know that her and I were a couple in high school, right?"

"Long time ago," I said.

"True, but hear me out here, Caes," Mike said, determined and earnest. "I never got over her, and the same could be said for her with me. When I got back, she sought me out and told me what was going on with her and her husband."

"And what was that?"

"Crazy shit, you wouldn't believe, but basically that they never should have gotten married but her old man wouldn't allow for a divorce, so Katie and her husband lived under the same roof as, you know, friends. She said he had a girlfriend or girlfriends, she didn't know exactly how many, but he was a real player, so why shouldn't she have someone, too?"

"And you're OK with that?"

Mike gusted a big breath and said, "I am Caes. This is Katie Donaghy we're talking about here, not some piece of ass who works in a whorehouse."

He flicked his wrist towards the bordello.

"Not everyone's as privileged as your precious Katie," I felt compelled to share.

"Yeah, well, I don't know about that," he said, haughty with the arrogance of someone who's never known disadvantage. "But she's the perfect woman from where I'm standing. Upstanding family and all that, too."

Cars were pulling in and out of the back parking lot of the bordello like it was a drive through.

"I assume I'll be invited to the wedding then."

Mike laughed whimsically. "Sure," he said.

"And I guess no one can say you're marrying her for the money."

Mike straightened his spine and turned toward me. "And here's the thing, though, Caes, I wasn't supposed to tell anyone this, but I can tell you, and you're going to love this, but you know that whack job my brother sent you to see?"

"Ira Zeiler?"

"Yeah, him. Apparently a real nut, that guy, but smart as shit. Anyway, he found the money Katie's husband had hidden."

"And how did he do that?"

"Who fucking knows. Some offshore operation he discovered going through Tuite's computer at work. You believe that?"

I didn't say anything.

"So he put it all back into Katie's account. You won't even fucking believe how much money we're talking about here."

"Good for Katie," I said.

"Fuck yeah."

"And her father must be pleased."

"Yeah," Mike said and then put his hand on my shoulder. "Too bad you didn't have anything to do with that. Not easy for guys like us to come across 100 grand."

"I'll say," I lied as the police lights lit up on the dash of cars and the hoods of patrol vehicles from all around the bordello. They crashed across the yard out front and through the parking lot out back. Men in FBI jackets and uniformed local officers stormed the small Victorian home with heavy weapons and search warrants on display. Ruckus - screams, busted down doors, broken glass - emanated out, but no shots were fired.

"Looks like they took your tip seriously," I said to Mike.

Mike nodded his head and shook my hand. "Seriously. Thanks, Caes. This is a huge deal for me."

"Happy to help."

Soon they were ushering out dangerous-looking men and barely dressed women and a passel of humiliated johns, one of whom appeared familiar. I took Mike's binoculars for a closer look.

"I thought Dick Donaghy spent his Saturday nights at church?"

Mike's jaw dropped. I thought of Dinny Tuite and smiled.

Chapter 36

On the day before Thanksgiving, I took Charlie to the town barber and got us matching haircuts. I hadn't had short hair since middle school, and it felt strange around my ears and the back of my neck; it also felt like a weight relieved and a change welcome. It also made me and Charlie look like father and son, or maybe the oldest and youngest siblings of the types of Irish families who had six or so kids over the course of a couple decades, like they used to do, back when I was a kid.

After that we went shopping at the local supermarket and an Italian groceria on the far end of town for a Mediterranean twist on a traditionally boring American holiday meal. We carried all the groceries back to the house, and Charlie would come early the next day to help prep for the feast. Brandy had invited one of her divorced girlfriends with two kids; Santi and Junior were bringing their families; Richie was coming with one of his girlfriends; and Mike would stop by for dessert after eating at his brother's house.

Mike had pulled some strings and got Dick Donaghy secretly released from the raid, which pissed me off to no end, but it did give me a card to play if the Dinny Tuite thing ever came back up again, though I doubted that it would. It also kept the Donaghy family from a lot of pain and humiliation, and that was something they deserved to be spared considering what a fucking prick they had for a patriarch.

Katie Donaghy showed up at the Inn that night before Thanksgiving. The place was packed on the night before a holiday, with some people home for a visit and everyone off of work the next day. There was a lot of drinking going on with a lot of reminiscing, so I helped Richie behind the bar. Katie looked heartbroken but poised, not really a widow but close enough. Her and Mike were lying low for the time being, which was smart, but they stole glances at each other often and their respective crowds mingled freely among the revelry that had the bar four deep and the register ringing long into the night.

It was fun to witness, and even be a part of, somewhat, and I certainly sensed what it was that made small towns attractive to so many, enough to reconcile my resentment but never buy in to the tenets of exclusivity that lurked beneath the surface. I'd live in that town on my own terms. We'd see for how long.

I'd thought at first to have our Thanksgiving dinner at the Inn, but having everyone - especially Brandy and Charlie - at the house seemed like the best idea. I'd been doing a ton of work on the house in my spare time of late, and hiring out labor to Junior and his crew, using some of my newfound cash, especially on the master bedroom in what was supposed to be the attic, and in one of the bedrooms on the floor above the landing. I'd gotten rid of all the old furniture and beds; ripped up old carpet and reset the floors; I'd also finished out the basement and had it set up with a TV and a game console for Charlie. The kitchen was no longer the fucking color of an avocado.

The new appliances in the kitchen were put to use early Thanksgiving morning as Charlie and I started the prep by removing the bones from an entire turkey, butterflying it into one long and flat piece, and setting it to brine in salt and sugar and aromatics. We mixed up a filling for the turkey of sausage and garlic and herbs held together with whipped eggs and some bread crumbs. After enough hours in the brine, I'd rinse the turkey and pat it dry, stuff it with the filling and roll it into a cylinder that I'd tie off with butcher string at two-inch intervals and then sear on all sides in a hot pan and finish off in the oven, coated at the very end with a honey and olive oil mixture for a golden glow.

Charlie made the stuffing all by himself, toasting chunks of day-old ciabatta and then scratching them lightly with cloves of raw garlic before sautéing sliced mushrooms and fennel bulb made paper thin through the use of a mandolin when his mother wasn't watching. He added some herbs and moistened the tossed ingredients with chicken stock before putting them into the new industrial oven just installed.

I taught Charlie how to clean chicken livers and make a pâté in a blender to be served as appetizers on crostini and topped with sliced shallots we pickled ourselves. We poached coarse polenta in whole milk until it was creamy and added mascarpone cheese and a topping of gorgonzola and crushed walnuts. Also on the side were roasted Brussels sprouts finished with a balsamic glaze and a sweet potato purée smacked with nutmeg and a touch of maple syrup. Our Hispanic guests brought empanadas for the appetizer course; Brandy provided the desserts and shopped for the necessary table settings that my mother's old pantry lacked. We'd drink Prosecco with the appetizers and Vino Nobile di Montepulciano with the main course and until everyone went home. That was the plan.

The big surprise would be that Brandy and Charlie were already home. I wasn't sure when I'd tell them, at some point before the meal I guess, but all the work I'd been doing on the house was for them. I was more comfortable in the flat above the Inn, and Brandy and Charlie needed a home. And better schools; and less stress. If anything would redeem our family, and remove our curse, this would be it. It would have taken three generations, but Charlie, the great grandson of the Sicilian matriarch who came to America to kill a man, would be the one to set the family straight again with the help of his mother and an uncle who'd never make the Hall of Fame, but who'd consider this a far greater honor.

Before the guests arrived, I cut out front to smoke a cigarette. It was a stunning late autumn day with sunlight bouncing off of everything and only a slight quiver in the trees. I drifted toward the street and sat on the curb in front of my house where I'd spent so much time as a kid. I ran a hand down the back of my neck, where phantom hair still existed, and felt the stillness surround me. A jet passed overhead. A train whistle blew. A motorcycle engine popped and bogged and grew louder as my father turned the corner of the big block on his old Triumph, the wind blowing back his hair and flapping the open cuffs of his jean jacket. He killed the engine a few houses down and glided to a stop right in front of me. I sat up straight just like I used to as a little boy when he came home, eager for attention and blessing. His face was leathery and rutted, but he looked good. Fit like the fighter he once was and always would be.

"And what's your story?" he asked and tussled my hair.

I couldn't wait to tell him.

Note from the Author

Word-of-mouth is crucial for any author to succeed. If you enjoyed *Black Irish Blues*, please leave a review online—anywhere you are able. Even if it's just a sentence or two. It would make all the difference and would be very much appreciated.

Thanks!

Andrew

About the Author

Andrew Cotto is the award-winning author of four novels and a regular contributor to *The New York Times*. Andrew has also written for *Parade, Men's Journal, Rolling Stone, Rachael Ray in Season, The Huffington Post, The Good Men Project, Condé Nast Traveler, Italy magazine, Maxim*, and more. He has an MFA in Creative Writing from The New School. He lives in Brooklyn, New York.

Thank you so much for reading one of **Andrew Cotto's** novels.

If you enjoyed our book, please check out our recommendation for your next great read!

Cucina Tipica by Andrew Cotto

"Whether you love Italy, dream of visiting it one day (like myself) or just want to enjoy an incredibly enjoyable book set in a beautiful part of the world, I thoroughly recommend this story as the best I have ever read!"

– *Midwest Book Review*

CPSIA information can be obtained
at www.ICGtesting.com
Printed in the USA
LVHW031602231220
674968LV00007B/392